In The Eye of The Storm

Sequel to *In The Eye of The Beholder*

by Sharon E. Cathcart

Copyright 2014, Sharon E. Cathcart

All Rights Reserved

This book or parts of it may not be reproduced in any form, stored in a retrieval system, or transmitted in any form by any means, without prior written permission of the author, except as provided by United States of America copyright law.

Cover design and author photo by James Courtney.

Printed in the United States of America by CreateSpace.

ISBN-13: 978-1497502673

Acknowledgments

There are always many people to thank when a book is finished. Of course, the fans of <u>In The Eye of The Beholder</u> are at the top of the list. So many wanted to know more of Claire's story, and it is my pleasure to share it here. Those who read the first book will recognize the tale as the first volume of Claire's journals in this one.

There are others whom I must thank as well. One of them is my high school French teacher, Miss Lois Sato. She passed away on January 7, 2013, at the age of 96. Miss Sato retired after my senior year; during my time under her tutelage, I learned a love for the French language and culture that will never leave me. When I decided to look up Miss Sato on the internet, to see whether or not she was still among the living, I learned that she had been interned at Camp Minidoka during World War II. Although she was older at the time of her family's internment, Miss Sato was my inspiration for the character of Grace Sakamoto.

I am also grateful to James Courtney, who not only designed the cover for this book and its predecessor, but who also accompanied me to an exhibit of Fauvist and modern art so that I could see some of the artwork in this story for myself.

Likewise, many thanks go to San Francisco mezzo-soprano Heidi L. Waterman. Not only is Heidi a brilliant singer and a great friend, she was an immense help in understanding the process of training a young opera singer -- right down to what might be an appropriate recital piece.

Thanks go also to my friends in the Treehouse and Bestseller Bound writing clubs, for their unfailing support and delightful company. You are all worth your weight in gold.

My husband, Jeff, has shown nearly boundless patience as I struggled to finish this book during a fairly significant health challenge in my life. If I might make a plea to my readers, please consider having your physician do a simple blood test to check your thyroid; far more people suffer from thyroid disorders than should. I am grateful for the support of family and friends as I learn how to live with Hashimoto's thyroiditis and all that goes with it -- including medication for the rest of my life.

Thanks also to my friends and colleagues at Humane Society Silicon Valley, where I volunteer. My special kitty friend, DiMaggio, was the inspiration for Clarice's finicky Lucifer. And yes, he has been adopted! Check out your local animal shelter if you are looking for a furry friend.

Finally, thanks to West End star Hadley Fraser, whose lovely performance of "Violets for Your Furs" gave me ideas for the moment in which a character's life changes unexpectedly -- and for the better.

Prologue
Clarice

Chapter 1

October 1948
San Francisco, California

Clarice waited quietly in Sam Wo's restaurant; her friends would be joining her any time now, just as they did the first Saturday of every month, for lunch.

When Clarice first sought permission to join some of the other senior class girls at their luncheon club, Daddy quizzed her extensively. Yet, it was her mother whose expression softened when Clarice mentioned the name of the funny little restaurant where the girls met.

"Let her go," Mommy had said. "It's a safe place."

So, once a month Clarice joined a few friends to dine in the restaurant. It was in a tall, narrow building on Washington Avenue; the food was delivered to the upper stories of the restaurant by dumbwaiter.

Clarice was pouring herself another cup of hot jasmine tea when she noticed an older Chinese man watching her from a corner table. She'd seen him in the restaurant many times, so she smiled. She was unsurprised when he smiled back but when he came over to the table just moments later, Clarice was not sure what to say.

He was taller than she'd thought, and nicely dressed. He studied her for a moment before speaking; his English was unaccented.

"You have your mother's eyes, but your face is just like your grandmother's." His eyes were sad, despite the smile he wore.

"Do you know my family?" Clarice was a little surprised.

"Ask Veronique," he said quietly. Then, he turned around and walked out of the restaurant just as Clarice's friends came in. If any of the lively girls noticed Clarice's distraction as they ate their egg foo yung and chop suey, they failed to remark on it.

Chapter 2

When Clarice got home, she was determined to have answers. It was time to remind Mommy of a long-ago promise she'd made.

However, Mommy demurred. It was only when Clarice told her about the Chinese man that she weakened. Her face wore a far-away look for a moment. She whispered "Samuel," and then turned her attention once again to her daughter.

"I still think you're too young," Veronique said.

"Mommy, you promised. And I want to know how you know a Chinese man."

Clarice twisted an auburn wave around her finger, her green eyes flashing. She reminded Veronique more of Claire with each passing day, not only physically but temperamentally. Even her fashionable hairdo, copied from one of the movie magazines in the beauty shop, seemed like something Claire might have done.

Veronique smiled at her daughter. "Yes, I promised. I also warned you that some of *Grand-mère*'s journals are a bit ... earthy. Are you sure you're ready?"

"Mommy, I'm seventeen years old and I've taken four years of French class. If I can't figure out a word, I'll ask you. And I know where babies come from. Ye gods."

Veronique was certain that the next thing the girl would do was roll her eyes. When she thought back to her own behavior at the same age, she would have done just that behind *Maman* and *Beau-Père*'s backs. Hard to believe that she had a daughter who was almost grown up.

"Very well then. And watch your language."

Veronique opened a hall closet and unlatched an old trunk. It was full of special memories and the treasures of her childhood: a stack of diaries; her treasured doll, Khadija, dressed in Persian attire; books; a yellow straw hat with faded green ribbons, a stuffed black horse that had been cuddled so many times her plush was worn in spots, a faded piece of rusty silk that contained a lock of black hair, a yellowed linen handkerchief that likewise contained a lock of reddish-brown -- nearly the same color as Clarice's curls.

Clarice pulled two chairs over to the trunk and sat down in one of them. Veronique sat down and took a deep breath as she drew out a child's diary.

"*Maman* and *Beau-Père* gave this to me. Of course, they told me it was from *Père Noël* -- Father Christmas. Maman and Papa kept journals. Ever since I got this little book, I have tried to do the same. Sometimes I find myself writing long stretches about things that happened many years ago, and forgetting to write about others. These older ones are theirs."

Clarice could hardly contain her eagerness. "Where should I begin?"

"Well, I think we should start with *Beau-Père*. And don't be shocked at what you read, my dear. That's the best warning I can give."

Veronique reached into the trunk again and took out a stack of books, carefully tied together in green ribbons. The first one was a copybook; the remainder were sketchbooks filled with *Beau-Père*'s beautiful drawings. She undid the ties and opened the topmost volume. *Beau-Père*'s artistic script filled the pages. Clarice had seen the sketchbooks many times; her step-grandfather's art was famous, and she had seen some of the earliest pieces. One hung on her bedroom wall. The journal was something else again.

"Here is the first one; bring it back to me when you are finished and I'll give you the next one. And don't tell Daddy yet. I've shared these journals with him and I'm not sure whether he'd approve."

"They're family stories, Mommy." Clarice, as predicted, rolled her eyes.

"I know, dear, but Daddy is rather more ... conventional ... than my side of the family were. As you will see."

Chapter 3

Clarice took the book upstairs to her room and closed the door. Her black cat, Lucifer, protested when she moved him from the pillows atop her bed and deposited him at the foot. Daddy had named the cat when he showed up on the back porch and refused to go away -- in no small part because Mommy and Clarice fed him. Lucifer was particular in his attentions; when he wanted to snuggle, he wanted only Clarice. He would sprawl on her lap, purring loudly, until he decided that he'd been there long enough and walked away, tail waving in the air. It would not do to pick up Lucifer, either; he wanted his feet on the floor unless it was his idea. Clarice adored him, and the feeling was mutual.

The dormer room had been Veronique's when the family first came to San Francisco, although it had been redecorated many times over the years. In a place of pride was a famous Rochambeau portrait of Clarice's maternal grandmother, done in Fauvist style. Claire Rochambeau had been the artist's model and muse, and Clarice had always been curious about this glamorous grandmother whom she had never met.

Mommy called the Rochambeau paintings the family legacy. Their occasional sale had helped keep the family afloat during the Great Depression and through the war years, although there was also money from a mysterious grandfather. Mommy's father, who died when she was just a little girl, had made careful investments abroad that still brought an income all of these years later.

Clarice sometimes tried to imagine what life had been like for Claire, the grandmother for whom she was named. She often wished that Claire were here to talk with; somehow it would have been easier to talk with an artist's model about the crush she had on Jimmy Aaron, her classmate -- and how much she wished he would ask her to a dance or even give her his fraternity pin. He was the captain of the football team: the Big Man on Campus. Every girl wanted Jimmy Aaron's pin. Or maybe even about Billy Wakefield, the boy at the stables where Clarice took riding lessons in Golden Gate Park. She couldn't imagine talking about Jimmy or Billy with Mommy, but she could talk to Claire's portrait and almost imagine the responses. Claire's face was serene under the cloud of astonishingly blue hair; Gilbert Rochambeau was one of the earliest Fauvists, and this little canvas was said to be the first of many studies he completed with Grand-mère.

Mommy had met Billy, of course; she'd taken Claire for her first riding lesson at the Polo Fields two years previously. Mommy rode as though she'd been born in the saddle. Claire loved it, but it was hard work. Billy was a patient teacher, but he was a cowboy. Claire didn't think that Mommy and Daddy would approve of a cowboy in the long run; Jimmy was planning to attend college and "make something of himself," even if he was never clear on exactly what that meant. Thus, it was Jimmy for whom Clarice set her cap.

Clarice also spent a lot of time talking to her imaginary grandmother about her best friend and former classmate, Grace Sakamoto. In 1942, when Clarice was eleven, Grace -- along with her entire family -- had been taken away to live in a camp at the Tanforan Race track. Grace and Clarice had been in the fifth grade together at the Presidio Elementary School. Veronique shopped at the Sakamotos' little grocery store.

Clarice recalled her confusion at the time; Mommy had said that the president signed an executive order saying that all Japanese people had to go live in camps; at the time Grace thought that this was like summer camp. How wrong she was.

Grace was American, just like Clarice. Mr. Sakamoto was born in Japan, but Mrs. Sakamoto was born in right in San Francisco. Clarice had been born in San Francisco as well, and for a time worried that she would be sent away. After all, Daddy was American, but Mommy was born in France. It seemed to her at the time that people who had only one parent born in America were being sent off and she was afraid for a long while until she got a little older and understood that it was only Japanese people. Veronique refused to shop at the Sakamotos' little store as long as the new family had it; she said she could shop somewhere else until the Sakamotos came back, that was all. She started buying her little tins of Smith's Rosebud Salve and other toiletries at the local Rexall Drug on Chestnut Street, and her groceries from another shop entirely.

After the war, Grace and her mother returned to San Francisco; her father, who had not been an old man, had become ill and died in the camp. Grace and her mother were not given the store back as everyone had hoped; they went to work in a dress shop in Japantown, sewing clothes late into the night. Clarice seldom saw her friend anymore; they did not attend the same high school. Clarice missed her; the girls from the monthly lunch club were nice enough, but Clarice didn't let any of them get too close to her. That presidential order had hurt more than just the Japanese people, Clarice reflected; she feared losing friends too much to be any good at making them after a while.

Even amongst the Saturday Restaurant Club girls, Clarice believed she would never find a friend as good as Grace.

Chapter 4

Clarice turned on her radio, the classical music low, and took off her shoes: fashionable ankle-strap wedges with Turkish toes. She always had music going and was particularly fond of opera. Her own singing voice was mature for her age; her instructor, Madame Rossellini, warned her to be careful of straining it.

"You have a rare gift," Madame told Clarice. "I want to see you taking a strong repertoire, but if you strain your voice, you will ruin it. I have never heard a young mezzo like you, Clarice, in my entire career. Perfect pitch and such presence!"

Clarice often wondered where that voice had come from; her mother was a brilliant violinist, but Daddy couldn't carry a tune in a bushel basket. She hoped that the answer lay in the journals. Propping up a couple of pillows behind her and tucking her feet up under the full skirt of her polka-dotted dress (the days of fabric rationing were over, and the dowdy straight skirts she and Mommy had both hated were long gone), she began to read as Lucifer curled up against her.

Part I
Gilbert

I

Claire asked me to write down my story; she and Erik were always making notes in their diaries, but I never did. No one would care about my story, or so I believed. But now, Claire says, people will want to know. Because of the paintings, she says. But those come much later in my tale.

I was born in the Camargue, in the south of France. All of the men in my family were gardians, riding the region's famous white horses to herd the equally famous black cattle. I, too, would have gone into that life. I learned to ride at a young age; not the elegant dressage that Claire studied, but the practical skills of a cattle rancher. It was a hard life, but a satisfying one.

I was the youngest of three children, and the only son. My eldest sister was married and lived in Marseilles; Helene seldom wrote and the distance was too far for frequent visits. My next oldest sister, Eugenie, was engaged to Francois Delacroix, a gardian from a nearby ranch. He was an astonishingly talented horseman, able to do tricks in the saddle and all manner of gymnastic riding. He taught some of his colleagues to perform similarly; they were great favorites at village festivals. It was at one of those fetes that Francois and Eugenie met. Everyone said they made a good-looking couple, she so fair and golden and he darkly handsome. My parents gave their consent to the betrothal and it seemed we would all be quite happy.

I had just celebrated my eighteenth birthday, and was looking forward to taking over the ranch from my aging father, when the accident occurred. I rode out to check the fences and a bird flushed out of a nearby bush. I was thrown from my horse, who reared in a panic and came down on my leg before I was able to move away. I can still remember my horror at seeing my bone sticking out through the leg of my trousers. I fainted, to my shame, and awoke in my bed. When my horse came back to the barn without me, the other gardians went to look for me and brought me home.

Our country doctor did his best, but he could not set my leg properly. It healed, to be sure, but shorter and with a hideously twisted scar. I had to order special shoes from the cobbler, and it was viewed as a given that I could not take over the ranch as I had hoped. That duty fell to Francois when he and Eugenie wed.

II

For the next ten years, Francois made my life on the ranch miserable. He envisioned himself as a gentleman farmer and spent vast sums on his appearance. At one point he seized on the idea that he needed a valet, and that this was the best way for me to "earn my keep." I learned to cut hair and clean clothes in order to keep a roof over my head and peace in the household. My parents both died during this time and left the ranch to Francois and Eugenie; I was now on sufferance in what should have been my own home, with only a small income from the estate. My hell was complete when my sister died in childbirth, along with the babe.

Francois was now lord of the manor, and I was nothing. I knew two trades: ranching and valet work. My leg denied me the first and, clad in whatever ill-fitting cast-off clothing Francois saw fit to give me, I'd no chance of finding another situation with the second. I was well and truly trapped.

As I re-read these words, I cannot help think of the old fairy tale about Cendrillon: Cinderella, she is called in English. It is an apt comparison to what my life was like.

Francois took advantage of every opportunity to mock me. He told me how ugly and stupid I was, and cuffed me at the slightest provocation. As though my limp were not bad enough, after a while I walked hunched over instead of standing up straight; it seemed the only way to protect myself against the frequent blows. I spent little time and care on my own appearance, for the energy seemed wasted. I had to focus on my survival; there was no room for vanity.

III

When Francois was summoned to Baincthun to serve as the unmarried Claire Delacroix's guardian, as noted in his late uncle Michel's will, he wasted no time. He sold the ranch without so much as a by-your-leave, gathered up his troupe of horsemen and his miserable valet, and rode north to serve as his cousin's charges d'affaires. It never occurred to him to ask whether Helene and I might wish to keep the ranch in the family; it was his to dispose of as he so chose.

As soon as he was decently able, Francois likewise exercised his rights in the north. He did not have to wait long.

Claire's fiancé, Philippe, was seriously injured in a barn fire. He was badly burned and lingered for some time. Claire nursed him diligently, and still would have married him despite his disfigurement; her love for him was deep. However, his pain eventually became too much for Philippe to bear and he poisoned himself with laudanum.

Upon Philippe's death, Francois sold the little stone farmhouse with its vineyard, Claire's jewelry, and all of the horses except one highly trained Friesian mare, Josephine, who was Claire's personal mount. He then packed Claire, with her clothing and her horse the only things to which she could still lay claim, off to Paris. There, he arranged a contract for the troupe at the Opera Garnier, including living quarters. Thus it was that Claire, an educated lady who had been betrothed to a moneyed man, became part of the theatrical demi-monde. Like me, she was trapped in circumstances beyond her control. The law required that her fortune be controlled by a male relative; as she had no husband, she was subject to Francois' whims.

I watched her from afar. She was kind to everyone, but kept mostly to herself. She always greeted me with a smiling "bonjour," but her air of melancholy was unrelieved except for when she rode Josephine. At those times, she seemed to forget time, place and circumstance; riding gave her a level of joy that no one could take from her. I watched her whenever the opportunity arose.

She would sometimes disappear for an hour or two; I later learned that she was caring for Erik's horse, Cesare. Claire never could resist an equine in need of her gentle treatment.

IV

Mine were not the only eyes that watched her from afar. There was another.

Erik LeMaître. The so-called "phantom of the opera." The man whom Claire married. How I envied him after a time. But that, again, is a story for later.

There came a day when Claire disappeared from the Opera Garnier, along with Josephine and her belongings. Francois put it about that she had run away with an opera patron, and that it was her fault that the troupe was sacked. He was plotting his revenge against her already; I should have been able to see it, even then.

One of the horsemen, Giraud, was found dead in Josephine's stall, strangled by an expert hand. Livid marks from a garrote stood out on his neck, although the weapon was never found. The crime was largely ignored by the gendarmerie; one more death in the demi-monde need only be ruled misadventure and none would think of it any further. It was not until much later that I learned Erik had killed Giraud after the latter tried to force himself upon Claire, and removed Claire from the opera house for her own safety.

V

I seldom had time to think of Claire again until one night in the little village of Montreuil-sur-Mer. Francois had, through what he considered fortunate circumstances, managed to capture Erik -- who was honeymooning with Claire in the village. Erik offered Francois a bribe to leave Claire alone after seeing a newspaper agony advertisement seeking her out, thus putting himself directly into harm's way.

I had never seen such an unfortunate and ravaged face as his. The discolored and malformed skin under the discarded mask were bad enough, but there were also whip scars that wove a lattice of pain on his back. There were new bruises as well. My god, how one human being could bear such cruelties was beyond me. My own misery was nothing to his.

When Erik saw me lurking in the shadows that night, he beckoned me closer and asked me to go to Claire. Although badly beaten, his clothing torn, he had an air of command about himself. He had a broken bit of porcelain mask and his wedding ring in hand to give to her as tokens; at first, I thought it was a trick. I had grown wary over time; the cruelties of Francois and his friends had taken their toll on me. But Erik was as good as his word; I found Claire beside herself with worry in a little cottage, cuddling a gangly tabby kitten she called Pierre.

When she told me that yes, she had married Erik and that she was resolved to return to that traveling fair to aid in his rescue, something swelled in my heart. This tiny woman, who stood only as high as my heart, had a courageous core of steel. I suddenly wished nothing more than to be her boldest and bravest chevalier: a knight of old.

"I am your man," I said to her, even as I was conscious of my ill-kempt clothes and my shabby appearance overall. In short, I did not look the part. But Claire didn't care; her concern was with Erik and so we went to him.

When we got back to the fair, Francois had goaded Erik into singing. I watched the faces of those who moments before had been taunting him. They stood transfixed, many of them weeping. I was not far from it myself; never before or since have I heard a voice of such beauty and purity. Erik stood, proud and arrogant, as the crowds melted away when he ceased his song.

When everyone had dispersed, I used one of Claire's hairpins to free Erik from the stallion cage in which Francois had locked him. He and Claire clung to one another, obviously in love and relieved that the other was safe.

Until Francois returned and threatened them both with his knife.

Something inside me broke at that point; I drew the pocket derringer I carried and shot him dead. No one would ever again threaten Claire or her loved ones if I could stop them.

VI

Claire set me on one of the horses to ride for Paris; Erik had friends there who would help us. I went willingly; I think I would have ridden into the mouth of hell at her bidding. Even if it meant living the life of a fugitive, it was worthwhile in my eyes.

It had been many years since I rode for hours at a time. As I rode, I found myself speculating on Erik and Claire's brief courtship. Their love for one another was apparent, but surely it could not have happened so quickly? Another flash of envy, and then I put those questions from my mind. There were more important matters that must be dealt with.

When I reached Madame Giry in Paris, I was exhausted. Yet, I insisted on returning to Montreuil-sur-Mer with Zareh, the Persian; I would not rest until I knew Claire was back in her home.

And such a home it turned out to be! That rococo townhouse in the Place des Vosges was like nothing I had ever seen, all white and gold filigree. I was used to far simpler surroundings than those in which I found myself. I am sure that I gawked like a country bumpkin. This was where Erik had hidden Claire in plain sight; the Marais was not that far from the opera house.

When Erik offered me a position as his valet and Claire's majordomo, as well as new clothing, a bath and a haircut, I was initially reluctant. However, I knew I was not only needed but safe with them. I had killed for Claire, and both she and her husband would protect my secret. I would also be near her; it was reward enough.

Erik directed me to burn the clothes I wore; the hated, cast-off garments from Francois were destroyed while I luxuriated in a hot bath. I had not felt truly clean in some time and bathed twice over from head to toe before I was satisfied. Erik gave me one of his fine suits, for we were of a size. I felt like a new man in the elegant garments.

Then the shave and haircut ... something I had done for myself for so long. I feared that Zareh's Parisian valet might make me look ridiculous, even though Erik was sophisticated and immaculate. His black hair swept back from his brow, smoothed with macassar oil, and he looked a perfect gentleman. That I might look the same did not occur to me until the neckcloth was removed and I stood to look in the mirror. A very fashionable Caesar haircut and a close shave ... a good suit of clothes. I hardly looked like myself.

I noticed Claire's blue eyes widen; for the first time in many years, a woman's gaze fell upon me and made me feel every inch a man.

My life changed completely from that day forward.

VII

I know how miserable my words sound as I write them. I imagine it is difficult to understand what my life had been like, and how little esteem I held for myself. I can only tell the story as it happened.

I suppose I should write about my friendship with Erik LeMaître. I was initially terrified of him; I would be a liar to say otherwise. He was a fearless assassin, and his word was law in the household. But then I realized that, like me, he had been subjected to abuse: only our response to it differed. I had been frightened and craven; Erik, for his part, was ruthless.

We were similar in height and build, as I have said; the suit he gave to me that night was the first well-cut clothing I had worn in years. He was determinedly fastidious in his person, almost as though compensating for the ravaged face he wore.

And ravaged it was. One side was handsome as a man might want, while the other was twisted and discolored by a port wine birthmark. The soft skin of one nostril was completely gone, and one eye was almost lidless. It was this disfigurement that he covered with his many masks. His eyes glittered green and his raven black hair swept back from his forehead. I kept it trimmed weekly to hide the clever hairpiece he wore; the ravaged tissues of his face extended to his scalp on that side.

Every time I saw Claire kiss Erik, unafraid of his appearance, my heart alternately swelled at her kindness and plummeted with jealousy and despair at the idea that I would find such a wife. There could surely not be a second woman like her anywhere on earth. I was equally certain that no woman would tolerate the horror of my twisted leg and the embarrassment of my limp.

VIII

I was more than a servant to both of them. Erik talked to me of his life in Persia, Russia and other far-off places. It was from him that I developed a previously dormant interest in art and literature. That Erik enjoined me to escort Claire to museums only fueled me further. I studied the sculptures, sketches and paintings closely so that I might understand color, proportion and light.

As I said, I was also Claire's majordomo. This position allowed me to spend time in her company whenever Erik was unavailable. He still grew distressed in public at times, so these opportunities were many. I would dress with particular care whenever we went out; I would never forget how Claire's eyes glowed the first time she saw me properly dressed, barbered and shaven. Erik's elegant appearance was my inspiration, but Claire's approval was my guiding light. I disliked admitting this to myself, but it was the truth nevertheless. I would not shame her by escorting her in anything less than the best-dressed state. Perhaps, I thought, some other woman might look upon me with similar admiration.

Erik was as vain as any dandy; I learned a great deal from his particularity. My razor was stropped so sharp that it could split a hair, just the same way that I maintained Erik's. He taught me how to tie my cravat in perfect folds and insisted that I be fashionably attired. He made sure that all three of us were perfectly turned out; so far as Erik was concerned, we were a reflection on him.

My warm little suite off the kitchen, chosen so that I need not negotiate the stairs several times a day, was an oasis. I would often wake to hear Claire in the kitchen making a pot of chocolate or toasting bread for breakfast. Our household was not shy of one another; she was usually in her wrapper with her hair loose. I often hurried to dress so that I might greet her. She would smile, wish me good morning, and share whatever she prepared. Sometimes she would touch my arm; the gentle caress was like fire to my love-starved skin.

The mornings when her lips were swollen and her throat red from Erik's kisses and love bites were the times that I envied him most. I often had to retire hastily to my room so that Claire would not see the physical response my body made to my imaginings; it was bad enough that such longings haunted me in the nighttime. I dreamed of making love to her far more often than I liked to admit. I ached for her in ways that I had never before imagined.

I am somewhat ashamed to confess that I occasionally slaked that longing in the brothels on Place Pigalle. Sometimes, I would even close my eyes and pretend that it was Claire in my arms instead of Mimi or Lulu. I doubt that the girls in those houses cared one way or another, so long as I left the right number of francs on the bedside table.

Above all, I was grateful to Erik and Claire. While I had indeed killed for them, I felt indebted. They rescued me from the miserable obscurity into which my life had tumbled and offered me a chance to start anew.

I was torn about the matter, of course. Like Claire, I was once a landed person in my own right. That our circumstances were reduced by the same man was not lost on me. If anything, it made me feel more deeply connected to her.

IX

I realize that I sound like a dog begging for scraps. In so many ways, that is indeed how it was. Having been subjected to so much unkindness, living in Erik and Claire's home was a restorative balm. I wanted what they had together for myself.

When Erik was occupied with his Persian friend, I would accompany Claire on her errands. As I have said, we visited museums. We likewise did the shopping and dined in cafes. On one occasion, at Antoinette Giry's invitation, we attended a ballet rehearsal. None of the girls recognized me as the skulking, miserable creature I had been, and they flirted quite openly with me. I could not explain to myself why none of them appealed to my lonely heart, to say nothing of my body. Yet, such was indeed the case. I wanted a woman like Claire, and she was not to be found among the simpering chorines.

Whores could be bought and paid for. Love could not.

So, I satisfied myself with my life in the LeMaître household, as peculiar as it might be. For the first time in many years, I had a home and not just a dwelling place.

I often joined Claire and Erik for shows at Montmartre's various clubs in the evening. Erik indulged in opium far more than I thought wise; I did not know then about the distress he endured over the household's planned move to England. He kept those thoughts to himself. It was on a night when Erik smoked far more than usual that the confrontation took place.

As I mentioned, ours was a very open and rather Bohemian household. I thought nothing of letting myself into Erik and Claire's boudoir to talk to her while she brushed her hair. That night, I took the brush from her and ran it through the long chestnut locks as I had seen Erik do so many times. Claire tilted her head back, her eyes closed; before I had a chance to consider my actions, I kissed her. Erik, who stood in the doorway of the bedroom, saw my folly.

I was sure I would be dismissed, but I was not. Worse, the next night Erik made me brush her hair while she stood in corset and stockings and he kissed her. He humiliated both of us, but the worst moment was when he said that Claire belonged to him, as though she were a horse or a suit of clothes. Claire dressed and stormed out of the house in a justifiable fit of anger. Erik refused my resignation when I offered it. I was furious with him; his treatment of me mattered not one whit as I had endured far worse, but his behavior toward Claire was not to be borne. My blood boiled as I left Claire's room in silence.

I was in my rooms off of the kitchen when Claire returned. Voices were raised and I came out to see her drop several coins at Erik's feet, saying that the wigmaker had paid well for her husband's property. Her locks had been cut just to her shoulders and arranged in a riot of curls held with pearl-headed pins. Her eyes were fiery with anger and defiance as she passed me to go upstairs, Erik hot on her heels. I had never seen anything or *anyone so beautiful in my life. And yet another pang of jealousy over the man who shared her bed.*

In every way but that, I acted as Claire's husband and escort. Even when we at last arrived in London, that changed little.

X

The ride on the ferry and train were uneventful, although I watched the French shore recede with an unexpected melancholy. I tried very hard to view the move as an adventure: a renaissance. Erik read aloud to us from Mr. Dickens' "David Copperfield," the first chapter of which was entitled "I am born." It seemed like a fitting tale, given that we were starting a new life in a new country.

It was not so easy as we might have hoped, sad to say. The English have long memories, and do not much care for the French -- unless they are looking for a fashionable ladies' maid. The shadow of the long-dead Napolèon Bonaparte was long there

Poor Claire was unprepared for how her life was altered by the move; truth to tell, all of us were except for Erik. He knew the immigrant life too well. Claire was hurt beyond belief by ladies who were not "at home" to her and who dared refer to themselves as her betters. This happened only once in my hearing; I ushered the termagant out of the house myself, promising to call the police if she did not depart at once. I had never been so angry in my life; how dare that woman insult a lady in her own home? And yet, that is just what she had done. The English pride themselves on their good manners, which I found ironic at the time.

I once again feared being sacked for my temerity in telling a guest to be gone. However, I could not keep my anger inside at the rudeness to Claire. That was the day I finally accepted that I was madly in love with another man's wife; once I admitted the truth to myself, I didn't know whether to laugh or cry. I consoled myself in courtship with Honor, Claire's English maid, whom I eventually married.

XI

The circumstances of Honor and me coming to know one another were singularly unpleasant. Claire's melancholia manifested itself so strongly that she became bedridden. She wished only to sleep. Erik gave orders that she never be left alone; melancholics often took their own lives. I later read, in Miss Florence Nightingale's "Notes on Nursing," that melancholics did better if they found company upon waking and if their rooms were well-lit via windows that could open for fresh air; Erik had made sure of that as well. I do not know whether he read Miss Nightingale, but that book became my Bible where Claire's care was concerned.

It was Erik's greatest fear that Claire would indeed suicide. He tried all he knew, even consulting a physician. When that man told him to kill Claire's beloved cat, Pierre, and get a child on her so that she would dote on the baby instead of her pet, I was surprised that Erik merely escorted him from the house instead of striking him. Heaven knows I considered it myself; I can only imagine how that must have felt to Claire's husband, with his violent tendencies. What kind of odd quackery demanded taking away a beloved friend as a means of so-called comfort? None that I could imagine, that is certain.

That evening, Erik carried Claire down to his music room and situated her on the divan. She looked so pale and wan, the entire household feared for her. In his desperation, Erik tried his one gift on her: music. Claire loved Chopin's <u>Polonaise in A Flat</u>, the so-called "Heroic," and Erik played it over and over again that evening. His virtuosity at the piano was undeniable; I stood in the doorway and watched him play the difficult piece flawlessly, tears streaming down his face.

After the sixth or seventh repeat, he closed the key cover and went to Claire, kneeling next to the divan. He slipped his arms around her waist and sobbed into her lap while she stroked his raven hair. I turned away myself, helpless to aid either of them in that dark and miserable hour.

XII

I took up drawing as a hobby, sketching museum exhibits and the like during Claire's and my outings; the days that she was of a mind to do anything must be taken advantage of, by Erik's decree. Most of my sketches were of Claire as she slept -- or as I remembered her in Paris. She ate so little now; her voluptuous curves turned to lines and angles. Honor lamented to me about how many of "Ma'am Claire's" skirts she took in at the waist.

Honor's sister Maggie, the family cook, took a turn at Claire's bedside one day; Honor and I took the opportunity to visit the market stalls near Covent Garden and take tea together in a restaurant. I found Honor very attractive, with her bright red curls and sparkling eyes. There was no denying that she was a pretty girl. She had flirted with me since her arrival in the household, which I naturally found flattering. As I would later tell Claire, Honor was a most appropriate match for me. My affection for my employer's wife was my secret burden to bear.

Honor and I were strolling arm-in-arm through the arcade when the stuffed toy horse caught my eye. It was made of soft black velvet and had beautiful glass eyes. Claire had left her black mare, Josephine, in France; this cuddly doll would perhaps bring her some comfort. I hurried to buy the toy before I could talk myself out of it, and then hastened home to give the stuffed pony to Claire. Honor raised an eyebrow as I took the stairs two at a time (a risky proposition, with my bad leg) and put the toy next to Claire on the bed.

"C'est Josephine," I whispered to her, and she wrapped her arms around the velvet horse. I touched her hair gently and left the room before I wept.

On one occasion, I took Claire to ice skate near the Tower of London, and on the omnibus to shop at Harrods. We had such a splendid day. I bought her a mug of tea and some roasted chestnuts, and for a few brief hours I could pretend that I was more than her valet. I like to think that these outings set her on the road to recovery, even though they tired her greatly.

Honor and I married not too long after that outing, eloping to Gretna Green and wedding over the anvil. Claire gave us gifts that she had ordered from Harrods as holiday surprises. I had a fine walking-stick with a blue glass knob, and Honor received an embroidered Spanish shawl.

XIII

Claire did not really begin to improve until Erik brought home the sad little chestnut mare whom she named Angel. As she helped Erik and me to grow with love, she did so now with the horse. Angel gave her a reason to rise from bed every day and be busy at something meaningful. Miss Nightingale was right about that, too.

Claire also developed a friendship with Doctor Sir Frederick Treves and his patient, Joseph Merrick. Treves had assisted Claire when she fell ill at the Covent Garden Opera, and realized that she was suffering from melancholia. He suggested that she meet Merrick as a way to feel useful; little did he realize that the two would become confidantes. She called on Merrick at the London Hospital several times. I met the gentleman only once before he died; he was kindly and intelligent, and so pleased to have a friend on whom he might pay a call himself, for Claire had given him her card and was "at home" to him.

Claire was badly hurt by how Treves treated Merrick in death. He used the unfortunate "elephant man's" remains to build his fortune, discussing Joseph's disease and exhibiting the man's bones to the public. While Merrick had joked about being kept in a great jar for people to look at, he was a devout Christian. Claire did not think it right that Treves should profit so from another man's suffering; in her most angry moments, she maintained that Treves was no better than the men who had caged Erik in the past. It will, then, be a surprise to learn that it was Treves who, at Claire's request, gave me a situation when she and Erik returned to France.

XIV

Treves told Erik that he needed warmer climes to stop the bleeding in his lungs. I, of course, presumed that Honor and I would join them. It was Erik who told me otherwise.

"She'll not do to Honor what I did to her, and I don't blame her," he said. "I took her away from everything she knew to a place where she spoke only some of the language and people hated her for her accent. I should have known better."

He put a hand on my shoulder then and looked me in the eye; his emerald gaze held me.

"Promise me, Rochambeau, that if Claire needs you, you will go to her."

"She'll have you," I replied.

"I'm dying, Gilbert, and I know it. No amount of warm air will change that. But before I leave this world, I'm going to give her the house she always wanted. I'm going to take her home."

"A terra cotta-walled house with blue shutters," I murmured. "She told me once that it was her dream."

"Indeed, mon ami. Now promise me."

I gave Erik my word. Shortly thereafter, Erik and Claire closed the house and sailed for France.

XV

So it was that Honor and I set up our own household. I went daily to the Treves' home to serve as general factotum and returned to my own hearth at night. I had only the most occasional letter from Erik or Claire; soon those stopped all together.

Honor and I had a good life together. She was kind and had a generous spirit. I could not complain about my marriage. It was certainly happier than many I saw around me.

I continued to write letters addressed to Claire, but they were seen by no one else. I kept them in my desk drawer, the stack growing regularly. I suppose I should have been ashamed, keeping a secret like that from my wife. Yet, I felt compelled to add to the little pile of clandestine correspondence.

Honor and I were married for almost four years when typhoid struck our London neighborhood. She nursed Maggie's daughter, Dolly, through it. Maggie's husband and son, Jeremy and Jamie, never caught it. Maggie herself was fine as well. The illness didn't touch me, either; it was Honor whom it struck. Maggie and I looked after her, and Doctor Treves even came to the house. He came out of the bedroom looking very grave indeed and could only shake his head at my inquiry.

I went into the room after seeing the doctor out. Maggie had just finished cutting Honor's hair to her chin; the fever was such that the heat and weight of it were too much. Her locks were dry and lank, and her eyes were hollow and dark.

"Give us a moment, Maggie," she said as her sister gathered up the two shorn red braids. Maggie nodded and left the room.

"Gil," she said, giving the soubriquet the hard English sound, "When I'm gone you need to go to her."

"I don't know what you mean," I said, genuinely confused.

"Go back to France, and to Ma'am Claire."

I stared at her.

She smiled wanly. "You think I didn't know? You've never loved me like you do her. You're good and kind, sure, and I'd ask for no better husband. But she'll need you. Now, go and let me sleep."

I left the room in astonishment. I had believed my secret to be so safe and yet she had always known.

Honor died in her sleep two days later. I mourned, with the rest of Honor's family. Doctor Treves was generous in allowing me time off. I decided that this particular chapter in my life had come to a close, and so I gave my notice a few weeks later. I had money put aside that would allow me to take my time about closing the little house Honor and I had shared. It also gave me time to plan.

XVI

I wrote to Claire; she did not write back. I wrote to Antoinette Giry, and it was she who told me by return post that Erik had died of pleurisy at home in Avignon. And still I heard nothing from Claire.

As it turned out, it was some months before I summoned the courage to go back to France for good. I had friends and family in London, and the leave-taking was more difficult than I'd anticipated. Jeremy drove me to the train station. From the train, I took the ferry and yet another train, reversing the journey that had brought me to England years before.

I went first to Paris; I wanted to have the latest suit and so on, so that I would make a good impression. I had grown a full beard, but the barber convinced me that the Van Dyck was the latest style and I was shaved accordingly. I carried the blue-knobbed walking stick Claire had given me some years back, and had a bespoke suit of brown Bath superfine that I knew suited my coloring. I was terrified at what I was about to do, and hoped that the suit, haircut and the like would serve as armor to bolster my nerves.

I caught the earliest train I could get for Avignon. I had a valise with my belongings and a sketchbook in my pocket. I had no firm plans, but knew I must take the risk I was about to assume. I couldn't concentrate enough to read or draw, and my stomach was too knotted to eat anything. What if she had forgotten me? What if she had someone else already? Was this trip folly after all?

I tried to focus on the countryside going by as the train sped southward, but my thoughts still raced. Sketching my fellow passengers was a temporary, albeit helpful, distraction. I noticed a number of the female passengers smiling in my direction, but did little more than give a polite nod in response.

When I at last arrived in Avignon, my first thought was to take lodgings and tidy up one last time before calling on Claire. Doing so unannounced frightened me, but not as much as being refused. I hoped that Claire would forgive my breach of etiquette.

The railway station attendant directed me to a boarding house. It was my good fortune that the landlady had a room to let with an eastern exposure; I would be able to paint if I felt so inclined. I had expanded my hobby from sketching to dabbling in oil paints and gouache. I had been told by several people that I had talent, and wanted to make a career for myself in the medium. I supplemented my income with portraits and landscapes here and there, but had new ideas I longed to try. The sun and colors of the Provençal countryside where I grew up inspired me.

I took the room for a week and paid the rent in advance. I brushed my dark brown suit clean and checked my appearance in the dressing table mirror. Would she even remember me? It had been five years since we had seen each other, and so much had happened to both of us.

I was ever conscious that Erik's shadow lay over us. I wondered how I would measure up with my courtship; I lacked Erik's seemingly infinite financial resources, just for a start. He had lavished Claire with clothing and jewels, baubles of all sorts. He had bought her a real horse, the beautiful Angel, to shake her from her melancholy. I had brought her a plush doll to remind her of the horse she had left behind. What fool's errand had I set for myself?

And yet, with all of the worldly goods Erik had laid at her feet, Claire had still succumbed to her misery. So many hours by her bedside, waiting in case she needed anything -- and to ensure that she remained alive -- had certainly shown me her emotional state. She was much more vulnerable than most people would ever know.

What if, by chance, she wanted more than material wealth? Erik's fortune would have gone to her; she had no need for further riches. What she needed was someone who loved her fragility as well as her strength. Surely I could give her that gift.

XVII

I remembered every detail about the last time I saw her. She came calling to the modest home Honor and I had made together, but did not remain long. Her blue coat, trimmed in silver fur, made her eyes blaze with color. Her abundant chestnut hair was arranged in a complicated coiffure of looping braids; sapphires sparkled in her pierced earlobes.

"I wanted to leave a card," she said, tugging one from her reticule. "I am always at home to both of you, mes amis."

Her eyes were bright with unshed tears.

"Erik is waiting in the carriage," she said after a moment. "I should go." She raised the fur-trimmed hood of her coat and opened the door.

"Au revoir," she said softly, and was gone like a delicately perfumed dream.

It was not lost on me that her farewell was "until we meet again."

I don't know how long I stood looking out the window as the LeMaître carriage moved out of sight. Honor put her arms around me and sighed; how could I ever have believed her ignorant of my feelings for Claire?

XVIII

Shaking myself from pointless reverie, I decided to take the attitude of "nothing ventured, nothing gained." I picked up my walking stick, set my hat carefully on my head, and set out to hire a conveyance.

In this, I failed miserably. No cab was to be found, and the owner of the railway station fly refused to take me to Widow LeMaître's home.

"Madame high-and-mighty will no more have you than me," he grumbled. "I'll not darken her drive again. Every unmarried man from miles around has tried to pay her court, not that it did them any good."

"Madame LeMaître and I are old friends," I replied. "If you will not take me to her home, surely you can show me which way to go."

He pointed up the road to a hill just outside of town. "That's where she lives. Look for the house with the blue shutters." He clucked his tongue to the horse and departed, his little wagon devoid of passengers.

How odd that he would refuse a fare, I thought as I set out up the road. I had come so far now; if I gave up to wait another day I might lose my resolve entirely. So, I walked.

The road was longer than it looked; I was tired and aching when I reached the foot of Claire's garden path. I drew in a deep breath. My clothes were dusty again, and I leaned heavily on my walking stick. A fool's errand for certain, and yet I had to press on. I came around a bend in the path and saw her house for the first time.

Just as Erik had promised her: a terra cotta and blue house. An arbor flanked it to the right; on the left were a barn and a pasture where her beloved horses grazed. The scene was peaceful and happy, as I had hoped Claire's life would be.

And then she was there, running along the stone pathway toward me. She wore a lavender calico dress and matching cloth espadrilles: a far cry from the silks and satins of Paris and London. Her dark chestnut hair hung loose to her waist; a fringe was cut across her forehead, emphasizing her blue eyes.

"Gilbert! Oh, my dear Gilbert!"

And then she stopped short. I stood quietly, mindful of my disheveled appearance and frightened of what I must confess to her. Claire's demeanor grew sedate as she smoothed her printed cotton skirt. I remembered that Erik had liked to see her dressed in that color; as always, his eye was perfect.

I asked if we might be seated as I had walked from town, and she took me to the arbor. She had a chaise longue there, covered in colorful cushions. I sat down and took off my jacket and hat; she sat beside me.

We exchanged pleasantries, and she asked me in to meet her daughter -- Erik's daughter -- Veronique. I took my old sketchbook from my pocket and gave it to her, watching her expression as she paged through the drawings. There were a few more lines around her eyes when she smiled, and she was woefully thin to my eyes despite having borne a child ... yet, she still held my heart captive.

She spent several moments looking at one of the sketches I had made while she slept. She had curled her hand under her cheek in a child-like attitude, and I had written a Shakespearean quote next to the drawing. She and Erik had taught me to speak English, and in that language I had written "Oh, that I were a glove upon that hand."

When she looked up at me, I confessed my love to her. And then she looked away.

I was crestfallen, my deepest fear realized.

"I had to try," I said softly, my eyes downcast.

And then I looked up at her again. Her beautiful eyes shone with emotion as she smiled and reached up to touch my hair. Her fingers caressed the back of my head as she ran them through my locks; I was doubly grateful that I was newly barbered.

Her lips parted ever so slightly and I lowered my mouth to hers. If this was a dream, I hoped never to wake. Her tongue slipped past my teeth to deepen the kiss, and her body melted against me. I broke away from her mouth and held her in my arms, stroking her hair. Oh, god ... to have Claire LeMaître trembling in my arms was beyond my wildest expectations.

"Let us go inside, my love," I said. "We have so much to talk about."

And that was how it began.

XIX

What I realized, with my return to the South of France, was that there is a certain magic of light and color there. It was only after I left the region where I was born and reared that I could truly appreciate it. The contrast with London's smoky grays could not have been greater.

I was not the only one to see this phenomenon. It took Van Gogh and Gauguin to Arles, just to name two. For my part, I was most fascinated with the work of Gustave Moreau.

I think that Moreau and his cadre of artists looked at those Provençal colors as impossible to capture; I know that I did. Instead of trying to mix the perfect tone to paint Claire's hair or dress, I would use something from my mind's eye, much as Matisse did when he made his wife's face a study in yellow, pink and green.

For her part, Claire was a most patient model. I was a little surprised; she seemed always, in the past, to need action and movement. Something in her had changed so in England; I sometimes despaired that she would ever be the same. Yet, she said that posing for me was a different kind of purpose, but a purpose nonetheless. Was it fair for me to doubt her?

She was model and muse to me, and eventually my wife. I think I may fairly say that I owe all that I am and that I have achieved to her quiet, gracious presence in my life.

That was the end of the first book. There was a folded piece of paper stuck into it at the end; Clarice carefully unfolded the fragile page and read Gilbert Rochambeau's letter to her grandmother. The artist's handwriting was clear and elegant, and she could almost hear his voice.

Dear Claire:

I watched your carriage drive away today, standing at the window until it was out of sight. There were so many things that I wanted to say to you, but you were gone.

I wanted to say those things when you stood in front of me, saying your farewells. You looked so beautiful in your blue cloak, its silver fox-furred hood lighting your eyes. Did I ever tell you how much your eyes reminded me of the Camargois sky?

No, I don't believe I ever did.

Your glorious chestnut-colored hair was styled in an elaborate coil of braids: very fashionable. Yet my fingers recall its weight as I held those locks to brush them.

And my lips recall the kiss I stole that night. Did you feel what I did?

I wanted to speak so many times when I escorted you around London or Paris. Restaurants, museums, shops; we went so many places together. I wanted to be much more than your majordomo, but you never knew.

You encouraged my drawing, but you never saw the dozens of sketches I made of you. Some were from memory, from the days in Paris. You riding your fine horse; I know how you have missed that black mare. Many of them were made while you lay ill; I feared for you, as did all the household.

I wanted to whisper to you then, but I said nothing. Instead, I brought a black velvet toy mare and gave her to you. Your quiet smile was thanks enough.

I understand so much better now how a sadness of the heart sickens the body. The doctor called your illness hysteria, said you were mad. How wrong he was. You have ever been sane, even in the darkest times. Perhaps I could have done more to ease your burdens; I will never know. But I did what I could.

I wanted to speak when you befriended Joseph Merrick, and when you railed at Doctor Treves, my benefactor thanks to you, for the way he treated Joseph in death.

I thought about speaking up when the English ladies decided not to receive you anymore. You tried so hard to make things right. I wished, many times, that we could all go back to France. Now you are going, and I am staying here.

I wanted to say something the night you made sure, for the first time in years, that I was dressed and barbered properly. Your eyes were the first to look upon me as a woman looks upon a man whom she admires.

I wanted to tell you whenever I watched your kindness to the people of the Opera Garnier. You never failed to smile and say a kind word, even though I knew your misery.

Oh yes, I knew your misery. I watched your cousin Francois ... my brother-in-law ... take everything you had. He did the same to my sister; she died giving birth to his child. He lived in my home, but made it clear I was there at his sufferance. I became a servant in the home that should have been mine: your cousin's valet. After all, how could a man with a twisted leg manage the affairs of a cattle ranch?

I watched Francois beggar and ruin you, and I could say nothing. He sold your home, just as he did mine. Damn those laws that say a man must control a woman's property. Those same laws gave my sister's inheritance to Francois; he squandered it all.

The closest I ever came to speaking my mind was the night I learned you were married, when Erik pressed his wedding ring into my hand and sent me to the little cottage where you awaited your newlywed husband's return. Francois even tried to take him from you.

That night, I said that I was your man. You presumed that I meant only to help you. The truth was, I meant that and more. I wanted to be a bold chevalier: a protector. Yet, you barely knew me; I was your cousin's valet, after all. It would have been unseemly to say more than I did on that night.

As it was, our lives were never the same.

Claire, I said nothing because I am a coward.

How could I say "I am in love with you," even as you were preparing to return to France with your dying husband? Erik was as good a friend to me as he could be, and you chose him.

How could I say "I have loved you from afar," without looking like a madman?

How could I consider casting myself at your feet and begging you to stay in London? And yet, that very thought crossed my mind as I watched your coach disappear.

How like you, in your compassion, to ensure that I would not be destitute in this strange land, since circumstances prevent me from going back to France with you.

There were times when you thought me so brave, Claire, but I am not. Only a craven would fail to speak these simple truths.

So, now I have done so, in a letter that no eyes but mine shall see. Perhaps one day, when I am in my dotage, I will tell my grandchildren about it. Perhaps, by then, I will be brave enough. I will live without you because I must, but your face will always live in my heart.

I am, your humble servant,
Gilbert Rochambeau

Clarice thought she had never read anything so sad or so romantic. Even though she knew some of what was in the letter from the journal's pages, she could not have imagined anything so plaintive as those words written from the heart. The journal was more like something for posterity; the letter was for love.

Chapter 5

Clarice closed the little volume and went back to find her mother.

"Can I have the next of Gilbert's journals, please?"

"What did you think of what you read?" Veronique replied.

"Well, it was so ... matter-of-fact. It was like he was reciting a tale for the newspaper man ... and not telling the whole story. But there was a letter in the back to Claire ... "

"Yes, I know. *Beau-Père* didn't leave another journal; he was too busy painting, I think, although there are notes in the sketch books about different events and paintings."

"I'd like to see some of them."

Veronique gave several sketch folios to her daughter, who took them to her room. There were many studies of Claire, the stone farmhouse and the animals. There are also many drawings of a masked man, virile and stern-looking ... and then some where his mask was off.

Clarice did not think she had ever seen anything more sad than how that same man looked with his face exposed to the world. He was scarred and disfigured, and watercolor sketches showed his skin to be discolored where the mask covered it: a purplish-red that Clarice had never seen on a person's skin.

There was one drawing that frightened Clarice the most, and that was of the man's back. It was crossed with lines that could only be whip-marks. She hurried to wipe away tears before they fell on the paper and caused any damage. How could anyone live through this, let alone trust another person?

This man in the drawings had to be her grandfather, Erik; Mommy had the same green eyes and straight black hair that Gilbert had put in the watercolors. The drawings raised even more curiosity in Clarice's mind.

Chapter 6

A few days later, Clarice decided to approach her mother about the matter.

"How much do you remember of your father, Mommy?"

"Very little. I was small when he died. I remember my *Oncle* Estefan and *Tante* Ornella were there, and that I loved him very much. *Maman* always felt distant to me; it was only years later that I understood why."

"He didn't scare you?"

"My papa, scare me? When he made me laugh, taught me to play the violin, and sang me to sleep? No, sweetheart. He didn't scare me. And if you refer to his face, because of Gilbert's drawings? No. He was just my papa, who happened to look like that. Of course, little girls always idolize their papas. You are no different. But I think you need to read some more to truly understand."

Veronique handed her two more books, with random bits of paper sticking out from them. "Here are *Maman*'s journals. Remember what I warned you of, Clarice. *Maman* was not shy about things."

Clarice rolled her eyes, just as Veronique expected she would. "I know about the birds and bees, Mommy. Remember? Anyway, what are these pieces of paper?"

"Notes from my father's own journals. There are only pages here and there, and *Maman* stuck them into her own diary."

Clarice took the stairs two at a time, eager to know more about the intriguing grandmother who had been loved by two men. Every now and again, she re-read the letter Gilbert had written. This was a kind of love that she had never known existed: across time and distance. She could hardly wait to know more.

She secretly hoped that Jimmy Aaron would one day send such a letter to her.

Over the course of the next few days, she finished the first book. That one had far more papers slipped into it. Clarice was occasionally embarrassed at her grandmother's writing; she was very frank about not only her courtship and marriage to Erik LeMaître, Clarice's grandfather, but also her confused feelings about Gilbert Rochambeau. As for Erik, it seemed to Clarice that her grandfather had little idea or experience of human kindness and that Claire was sometimes beyond his ken. All the same, he cared deeply for her, and vice versa.

The hardest parts for Clarice to understand had to do with Claire's mental illness. Gilbert had touched on it in his brief journal as well. Mommy had said that sometimes *Grand-mère* was unwell, but she'd never elaborated. Claire's melancholy was something that Clarice could understand well enough, although she was able to keep her sadness in check and function normally. This was the blessing of her youth. From Clarice's understanding, though, women who were as ill as Claire would have been locked away. *Grand-mère* had been lucky to have two such understanding husbands.

Grand-mère had indeed been very frank about lovemaking; Mommy was not kidding. Clarice had more than once found herself blushing at descriptions of what Claire and Erik had got up to. She had even imagined doing some of those things with Jimmy Aaron. The idea excited her, even though she believed strongly that some things should wait until marriage and couldn't imagine Jimmy Aaron doing some of the things she'd read. *Grand-mère* and Erik had not held with such conventions, that much was clear.

A few days later, she picked up the second book. Unlike the first volume, there was only one slip of paper in it. Clarice settled in to read more about her grandmother's life.

Part II
Claire

I

I must write some things about this family, and the so-called Phantom of the Opera. Erik LeMaître, Veronique's father, who died when she was small. My first husband.

He was tall and black-haired, a gifted musician and composer who could make up tunes on a whim. Before the pleurisy that killed him stole his lungs and voice, he was a brilliant operatic tenor whose voice could wring tears from his listeners' eyes. I am not exaggerating; I saw it happen. Our house was always filled with music. Erik was Veronique's first violin teacher; her musical talent came from him and was Erik's greatest legacy. Erik gave her his black hair and green eyes, a striking combination.

Erik was also a notorious strangler, a murderer, and a kidnapper. A journalist named Gaston Leroux documented all of that, although not everything in his book is true. He told the story he wanted to tell, no matter who might have been hurt or slandered in the process. But that is a tale for later.

In my younger days, I was chestnut-haired; nowadays, my hair is white as Alpine snow. I was an accomplished horsewoman and, if Erik's journals are any measure, a healer of those who were psychologically or physically damaged. Heaven knows, Erik LeMaître was both.

Gilbert Rochambeau was my second husband. A handsome man with brown eyes and hair the deep gold of an old Roman coin, he walked with a cane because of a badly-set broken leg in his youth. He loved me passionately, and had done for years — even while I was married to Erik. Gilbert was a gentle man with a core of granite. That, however, was something that I learned later.

Erik and I returned to France after he was advised to live in a warmer climate. He had begun to cough blood, and Doctor Treves thought that the warmer air might do him good. He was a fractious patient, to say the least.

Erik worked with an old friend from his Persian days, Zareh, to purchase a little farmhouse outside of Avignon, and arranged to have it painted just as I had always wished: terra cotta with blue shutters. There were pasture and barn for the horses, and a flower garden that we cultivated together. Erik proved surprisingly skilled at caring for the horses and the plants, although he would have a coughing spell if he worked for too long at a time. He was too stubborn to let me do it all by myself; for my part, I had learned long ago that it was pointless to argue with him.

Fortunately, his knowledge of herbal medicines was put to outstanding use. Tinctures and tisanes were always brewing in the kitchen so that he might be more comfortable. I was cautiously optimistic that Doctor Treves was right and that the Provençal weather would prove efficacious. Each day that Erik was out-of-doors, garbed in cord trousers, boots, a loose linen shirt and heavy gloves, working in the barn or the yard, I considered it to be a victory. His aristocratically pale skin darkened in the sun; he looked significantly more healthy, although that appearance was deceiving.

At first, our nights were just as intimate as before; I found Erik as hypnotic and irresistible as I had from the first -- perhaps even more-so. His touch set me aflame. There was more than one day when our work was interrupted by al fresco lovemaking. A caress in passing inevitably turned to a kiss, and then coupling. I was more tentative in my lovemaking after a while, fearing to bring on a coughing spell, but I still went to him willingly whenever he was able. I never initiated the act myself, which was a change. After a while, Erik didn't offer either.

II

The day the Rom came calling changed our quiet lives once more.

They stopped their caravan at the foot of our drive, and a woman came to the door. Her accent was strange to me, but Erik obviously recognized it. He went outside, mask in place, and spoke to the woman in a language I did not understand.

While Erik talked with the woman, I went outside with a bucket full of cool water to offer the horse hitched to the front of the caravan. He was a small, sturdy gelding, pied black and white, with a thick mane and tail. Long "feathers" covered his hooves, just like they did on Josephine.

I stroked the horse's forehead between his eyes, speaking in a soothing tone. I hadn't looked up at the driver, so I was surprised when he spoke to me.

"Nais tuke. Thank you. It is good of you to consider him. He is called Lladro."

I glanced up, but the man had looked away and was concentrating on the discussion at the other end of the wagon.

"There is water for you, too," I replied. "And food if you would like it. I also have some pots that need repair ... "

"We are not ferari, we are grastari." His tone was dismissive.

I did not understand the strange words, of course. I left the bucket of water and walked back toward the house. Erik called my name and beckoned me to join him.

"Mi romni, Claire," he said.

"Me som Ornella," the olive-skinned woman replied. Her black eyes flicked up and down, examining me.

"I'm sorry. I don't understand."

"Her name is Ornella," Erik translated. "She and her nephew are horse traders."

"None of ours are for sale."

"I have told her that. She and her nephew seek permission to camp here tonight on the way to their next fair," Erik explained. "She saw how well our horses looked and thought the grazing might be good."

I nodded. I had learned enough of life by now that fear and prejudice did not enter into my thought process. I did not believe the old wives' tales about the traveling folk.

"You are welcome here," I said.

Erik translated. I would later learn that both Ornella was as fluent in French as her nephew.

"Estefan," Ornella shouted, and the caravan driver hopped down to join us.

III

That was the moment when shock set in. But for the swarthier cast of his skin, pencil-thin mustache and lack of deformity, he could have been one of Erik's family. The resemblance was particularly marked as Erik's skin had taken on golden tones from the Provençal sun.

The two of them stared at each other and Erik again spoke in the unusual language. The only word I understood was Rouen, the city of Erik's birth.

"Plal?" Estefan shook his head and then spoke to Ornella.

Erik took me off a ways.

"It seems that a certain stonecutter in Rouen, my father, managed to get himself a child on one of the Rom," he said. "Probably on the night he sold me to them. That woman was Ornella's sister. She's dead."

I was dumbfounded.

"So, Estefan is your brother?" I was surprised, but could not say why given my earlier observation.

"Half-brother. But yes, that appears to be the case."

"Well, tell them that family is welcome here."

Erik spoke again. Ornella's response was emphatic.

"Gadje gadjense, Rom romense."

"Non-gypsies together, Rom together." Erik sighed.

I went back into the house but watched through the window. Estefan shook his head in annoyance and left Erik and Ornella to their discussion. He knocked at the door and I let him in.

"Please, mi phen, may I have some water?"

His French was flawless, but I did not understand the foreign word. I asked what it meant.

"Phen, it means sister." *He drank the proffered water.* "There is no doubt that this Erik is my brother. You are his wife, and my sister."

He was breathtakingly handsome and exotic. His black hair was pulled back tight in a braid; a gold silk scarf covered it. I would later learn that, unbound, it rippled past his broad shoulders.

"What is the word for brother?" *I asked.*

"Plal."

That was the word he had used outside. Now I understood. Eventually, I came to know many Romany words, although I was never fluent.

IV

I never told Ornella or Estefan that I knew Erik was dying, but somehow they sensed it. They asked leave to camp in our pasture whenever they were in the area and both of them helped around the property. Erik did what he could, but often ended coughing and irate. He was just as irascible as ever.

Ornella had many teas and tinctures that she mixed in the vardo and brought to the house. I never knew what was in them, but they seemed to help Erik more than anything the town's doctor, or Erik's own recipes, could provide.

One afternoon, Ornella eyed me speculatively.

"Come," she said. "We must talk alone."

She took me into the vardo and offered me a cushioned bench seat.

"You are not making love with him," she said bluntly.

I could feel the heat rise in my cheeks.

"Claire, I know you do not lack the desire. I see how you watch Estefan, and I know it is because you see Erik in him."

I was mortified, but could only nod. Ornella spoke the truth.

"I'm afraid," I whispered.

"Of what?"

"Hurting him. Killing him."

"God preserve me, Claire," Ornella rolled her eyes. "Bedding Erik won't kill him."

She studied me intently.

"You think he doesn't want you anymore."

My eyes widened.

"How do you know that?"

"I am *fortunari*: a fortune teller. It is my job to know," she chuckled. "I have a bit of the sight, sure, but it only wants human eyes to see how you look at Erik. You follow his every move. Only a fool could not see the passion you feel for him. He fears to hurt you, too, girl. He fears to embarrass himself: that his illness will rob him of his manhood."

She stood up and pulled jars from cupboards and drawers.

"Tonight, we will have a *pachiv*: a party. There will be food and dancing. And music. There must be music. Estefan will play his guitar. I will ask Erik to play the violin. Wait here."

I remained in the vardo, feeling as though I'd stepped into a hurricane. I heard Ornella talking to Estefan outside; I still knew very little Romani and could not follow the conversation.

Estefan came into the vardo and pulled some clothing from a trunk. With a nod to me and a knowing smile to his aunt as she came back, he was gone.

"Now, *mi phen*," she said, "We have work to do."

V

I was a nervous wreck as Ornella put the finishing touches to my toilette. I'd passed the afternoon inside the vardo with her. A foul-smelling herbal concoction left my chestnut brown hair glinting with red tones once it was rinsed out. Ornella tied it up with multi-colored strips of cloth and, when it was dry, brushed it out so that waves rippled almost to my waist.

I wore a loose cotton blouse that slipped down over my shoulders, a wide belt and a russet-colored silk skirt that shown gold and red as the light played over it. Ornella's clothes fit well; I was still far thinner than before.

Ornella fastened heavy gold hoops into my pierced earlobes, then pulled out her paints. Kohl rimmed my upper and lower eyelids and she brushed some of it onto my lashes. The contents of a red pot tinted my mouth; a touch of exotic perfume scented my skin.

"There." Ornella held up her small mirror.

The woman in the reflection looked nothing like me; she was neither tired nor frightened.

"Now, I will come for you. I will take the bokoli, You must bring this." She handed me a flask. "Share it with Erik."

I nodded, and she left the vardo.

Outside, Erik and Estefan had cleared a space and built a campfire. Dusk was gathering and, even though it was a late summer night, it could still grow chill.

"Come," I heard Ornella say. "I would hear a pachivaka djili: a party song. Tonight we celebrate."

Erik started a melody on his Chanot violin, the tune wild and melancholy in its minor key. Estefan joined in on his guitar; the music was haunting and seductive as I swayed in time.

Shoes! I had no shoes. When Ornella reentered the vardo, I whispered my concern.

"I know, mi phen. Just come with me." She picked up the tray of bokoli on which we would feast, and I followed her out to the firelit circle.

I almost dropped the flask when I saw Erik. Estefan had obviously provided his attire; I wondered how he had convinced my husband to wear the snug leather trousers, open shirt and high boots, to say nothing of the russet silk sash at his waist. It was clearly cut from the same bolt as the skirt I wore.

The firelight's glow set his pale leather mask alight with color; his eyes were closed as he focused only on the rondo he coaxed from the violin's strings. The Chanot had a sound like no other violin I had heard before or since, rich and full. Erik's elegant fingers played over the strings that he caressed with the bow; his focus was only on the music that came forth at his bidding.

I was suffused with desire, but stood stupidly rooted to the spot. Then, just as I had in the vardo, I moved in time to the music. I swayed over to where the two men perched on their low stools, long legs extended toward the fire. My skirt rustled with every movement.

Erik had once named me a hoyden, and it was that buried part of me that I called upon to return. I moved behind Erik and whispered into his left ear, my breath warm on his bare cheek.

"How beautifully you play, mi rom."

"Mmm, mi romni," he sighed, not missing a note.

I drew my nails across his shoulders as I stepped closer to the firelight. I carefully set the flask down.

"Ornella, perhaps we should dance for these fine musicians."

It was only then that Erik opened his eyes.

Ornella and I danced, moving in any way that the music made us feel. Estefan's guitar chords sent a rhythmic thrumming through my body, while Erik's violin was a counterpoint that whispered desire.

He never took his eyes from me as he stood up and moved closer. Not one note did he miss as his eyes held mine, the seducer's green gaze holding me in thrall. His power and control, both as musician and man, were undeniable.

Estefan stopped playing just seconds before Erik, leaving the two of us standing in the firelight. The air between us was tense with desire.

"Such music deserves reward," Ornella said at last. She handed me a plate of bokoli and the flask.

I followed Erik to the stool where he had sat. He put his violin in the case and seated himself. I straddled him, my back to the fire.

I plucked a bit of bokoli from the plate and held it to his lips. His eyes never left mine as he guided my fingers into his mouth. He swallowed the meat and licked my fingers clean. His tongue flicked out to tease the delta of flesh between my thumb and forefinger and I shivered. There was no mistaking his intent.

The first time we'd dined together, Erik had fed me. That offering was gentle and romantic. Tonight, our mutual intent was unmistakable, playing out in every gesture ... every bite.

I uncorked the flask and drank of it; the liqueur tasted of honey and herbs. I passed it to Erik who finished it. When he kissed me, I could taste the sweet nectar on his tongue. His fingers entwined in my hair as he moved his lips up my jaw and to my ear.

"Claire." His whisper was ragged.

"Mmm," was all I could manage as I slipped my hands inside his shirt.

"Wrap your legs around my waist."

I did as I was told and he stood up, his arms around me.

"Use the vardo, mi plal," Estefan said. "We'll see you in the morning."

VI

Erik carried me into the wagon and deposited me on the wide bed at the front.

"God, Erik," I moaned.

He was so beautiful, standing over me. He stripped off his mask and bent down to me.

"She made you a Rom bride," he whispered. "The clothes, the hennaed hair ... even the honey liqueur. How ..."

"Then you should claim your right as a husband," I whispered in return.

Erik's eyes darkened and he smiled slowly. He stripped out of the shirt and stood before me in sash, boots and leather trousers that strained with his desire.

"Ah, mi romni," his voice took on a different accent as he spoke the Rom words. "Indeed, I shall."

The silk skirt made it very easy to reposition me so that my legs hung over the edge of the bed. He tugged my drawers away and they soon joined the discarded shirt on the floor.

I watched as my elegant, aristocratic French husband became the Rom bridegroom. His posture, attitude and voice all changed before my eyes. He seemed feral as he knelt between my knees and pushed my skirt up.

His tongue touched my flesh and teased me until I ached for release. I was at the edge of climax when he moved away, untied the sash at his waist and unbuttoned his trousers. His sex was hard with desire.

"Prepare to accept your bridegroom," he growled, and thrust deep within me.

My hips bucked, trying to catch his rhythm. When he took hold of my ankles and draped them over his shoulders, pushing deeper inside me, I cried aloud. This was a coupling born as much of animal desire as of love, and there was nothing fearful or tentative about it.

Erik's climax pushed him deeper inside me. He gasped as he withdrew, his manhood limp against the leather fly. He sat down on the edge of the bed and pulled off boots and pants.

"Undress," he whispered. His eyes still held a feral glow.

I did as he directed and leaned back on the bed.

Erik collected the silk sash from the floor.

"Now, my gypsy bride," he mused, "what shall we do with this?"

He trailed the fabric across my nipples and took one of my hands.

"Should we bind your pretty wrists? I saw no bracelets tonight. Surely your wrists should be decorated for your gypsy king." He tongued my wrist gently and I writhed at the sensation.

"Or perhaps we should cover those kohl-rimmed eyes," here he paused to kiss my eyebrow, "so that you do not know what is coming next."

I shivered.

"Maybe we will use it to tie back that beautiful hair, now that you are the respected bride of a Rom." He dugs his fingers into my tresses as he drew the silk across my nipples.

His every touch set my skin aflame.

"What will we do, mi romni?"

I instinctively understood how I had to answer.

"As you will, mi rom." I had been given the role of seducing bride; his part was to take command.

"You are mine to command, now and always." His voice was warm against my ear. He dropped the sash once again to the floor, where it was soon forgotten.

He kissed his way down my body to my sex and set his mouth to me again. He held my thighs firmly; I was unable to escape. My climax was strong and inevitable.

When Erik kissed me, I tasted both of our essences on his tongue. When he slid into my wet and throbbing sex, I welcomed him, pulling him deeper by wrapping my legs around his back.

"Tonight," he whispered in my ear, "I will take you again and again. Tonight, I will get a child on you."

"Yes, oh god, yes," I murmured.

We climaxed together. When I opened my eyes, I saw the purest love I had ever known. He loosed my hands and I dug them into his black hair to pull his face to me for a kiss.

"We are the grastari," he whispered. "Horse traders. Once you showed me how you train a stallion. Tame me if you dare."

He reclined on the bed.

"Erik, you will break us both."

"No, mi romni. Tonight is ours." He beckoned. "Tame me ..."

I feathered my fingers across the port-wine stain on his right cheek, down the damaged nose, across the maddeningly perfect mouth. Down his chin to his chest.

"Turn over," I directed, and he did so. Even after all this time, the whip scars across his back sickened me.

I took up the same perfumed oil with which Ornella had anointed me earlier and dabbed a bit onto my fingertips.

"I must heal your hurts and teach you to trust me."

I caressed each scar gently, leaving a spice-scented trail. I had often avoided touching these grisly reminders of Erik's past, but tonight was a time for new beginnings. My lips traced what my fingers had begun, and I kissed each white line.

"No one will ever hurt you again," I murmured. "You are safe with me."

I leaned in to whisper in Erik's ear.

"You are loved."

"It's important to gain trust," I whispered. "On your back again, my love."

Erik turned over; all of the tension he had displayed of late seemed to have disappeared. I fed him another bit of bokoli, taking a piece for myself as well. I wiped my fingers clean and then continued my gentle exploration of his body. I ran my hands down his arms and legs, just as I did when checking a horse's limbs. With each touch, he groaned in pleasure and his arousal was soon apparent again.

"Will you let me mount you? Ride you?" I whispered as I straddled him, guiding him in.

Erik's response was to pull me closer and wrap his arms around me as he plunged deep. I did not imagine the tears we both shed as we climaxed yet again and fell asleep in each other's arms.

VII

When we awoke, we were covered in a warm perina blanket. The clothes we'd scattered on the vardo floor had been tidied away; Erik's and my dressing gowns and house shoes were on the table next to his mask. Whichever of the two Rom had cleaned up after us had been so stealthy that we never noticed them.

Erik held me close to him.

"I was so shocked when you came out last night," he whispered. "I had never seen you that way. You were magical."

"And you!" I turned to face him. "The gypsy violinist ... you were ... "

Words failed me.

"Yes?" A smile played over his lips.

"You were a god and a demon, all at once," I finished.

He brushed my hair out of my eyes and kissed me tenderly.

"I must remember to thank Ornella for the pachiv," he said. "To have another wedding night with you healthy instead of ailing was a gift I shall treasure always."

I thought back to our actual wedding at Montreuil-sur-Mer. Erik had looked so handsome in his morning suit, and I wore an ivory costume he had commissioned for me from a favorite dressmaker. Then, as now, I had not known quite what I was getting into when I donned the clothes given to me. And then I had become ill, fevered and coughing. Just as my health improved, Francois had taken Erik ... but I didn't want to think about that time.

Erik gently traced my abdomen with a long, elegant finger.

"I meant it," he said. "I will give you a child."

Given how many times we had made love, with and without precautions, I was doubtful. I presumed myself infertile and was not terribly concerned one way or the other.

"Time will tell, mi rom," I replied, curling up against him.

Clarice closed the book. She was embarrassed by what she had read, and yet she found it exciting. She tried to imagine Jimmy Aaron as a Gypsy bridegroom and herself as his wife, but could not bring the image into focus. She tried to imagine him being passionate about anything besides football, and could not.

It seemed to her that Claire was forever teaching Erik how to trust. Clarice had seen a great deal of patience and love in the description of how her grandmother had lovingly touched each part of Erik's damaged face, each scar, as they found their love for one another again. There was a life lesson here, to be certain.

Chapter 7

Studies and examinations took up time that Clarice would otherwise have spent in leisure reading, and there was a big school dance for the homecoming game. She hoped that Jimmy Aaron would ask her to go with him, and was heartbroken when he did not.

Worse, he gave his fraternity pin to Eleanor Fountain. Eleanor was a cheerleader, with long blonde hair and (if Clarice did say so herself), not an original thought in her head.

Melissa Jenks, one of the girls in the Saturday Restaurant Club, told Clarice that she was too smart for Jimmy Aaron anyway.

"He doesn't want a girl who can think rings around him, Clarice. Face it; Eleanor Fountain is not the sharpest tool in the drawer, and that suits him just fine. There's someone better out there for you."

It didn't make the hurt go away, though. Melissa had a fellow, Joey, who worshipped her. Clarice had no one. And, to be honest, the more of *Grand-mère*'s journal she read, the more she wanted to have a fellow who made her feel as Claire had about Erik.

Clarice had a Saturday riding lesson with Billy, who remarked that she did not seem quite herself. She could hardly tell him about Jimmy, so she just said she wasn't feeling well. The young cowboy gave her a knowing look, but did not press the issue. He took her out for her lesson, and then showed her some of the reining tricks he knew; he could make his little grey horse, Spirit, do just about anything. By the end of her lesson, Clarice was at least smiling again.

Chapter 8

The following week, Mommy dropped Claire off for her lesson, so she was a little early. As she entered the barn, looking for Billy, she heard someone singing at the end of the aisle. Tiptoeing through the barn, she followed the sound -- only to discover that the beautiful baritone belonged to Billy himself.

"I had no idea you sang," she said quietly.

Billy blushed to the roots of his thick blond hair.

"Nothing like you do. Nothing fancy like opera. Just songs I like."

"Will you sing something for me, Billy?"

He nodded. "This is my mother's favorite," he said, and began to sing "Violets for Your Furs," a Billie Holiday song that was popular a few years previously. His voice was beautiful; the song suited him well. He looked deeply into Clarice's eyes as he sang the song; she was captivated.

This must be what *Grand-mère* felt the first time she heard Erik sing, Clarice thought, her eyes never leaving Billy's gaze as he finished the song.

He leaned forward and kissed her gently on the mouth. Then, he kissed her again, firmly.

They stepped away from one another, each looking into the other's eyes. Billy's were a startling pale blue with dark rings around the iris. His face wore an expression that Clarice had never seen on a boy before.

For her part, Clarice could feel the flush rising to her cheeks. She suddenly understood exactly what *Grand-mère* had meant about some men's kisses. She didn't think she could ever have eyes for Jimmy Aaron again.

"Clarice," Billy said, "I wonder if you would allow me to take you out some time."

"Of course," she breathed.

The riding lesson seemed all too short that day.

Veronique studied Clarice's face when she picked her up.

"What happened today," she asked as she drove back to Union Street.

"Oh, Mommy. I ... Billy ... oh, Mommy. I never realized how ..."

Veronique smiled knowingly. "I think I understand better than you know, my dear. I was your age once. Billy is a nice young man, and he works hard. Those are important qualities; I wish I'd realized that sooner."

"He wants to take me out, Mommy."

"Do you want to go?"

"Oh, yes. I do. And guess what, Mommy? He sings."

"Does he?"

"He sang 'Violets for Your Furs' to me. It was beautiful."

"Mmm." Veronique knew the song; it was about a young couple falling in love during a Manhattan winter. "That is a beautiful song."

Clarice felt like she was floating on air for the rest of the day, and it seemed as though her next riding lesson was years away instead of a week. She had a hard time concentrating on her studies and realized that there was only one book she felt like reading.

Clarice picked up *Grand-mère*'s journal and opened it to the page she had marked. She had no doubt that Claire would know exactly what Billy made her feel.

VII

Over time, Ornella and Estefan often camped in our pasture. There came a day about three months after the pachiv when I was doubly glad of it. Erik had gone into town to pick up our order from the greengrocer and Ornella accompanied him. No one would harass her in Erik's presence; she would be able to collect supplies for the next part of their journey.

I rode out on Angel, bareback, down to the little stream that ran along the back of our property. I missed my regular dressage routine and settled for riding one of the horses each day. It was one of my greatest joys.

Angel was still excitable; her Arabian blood and history of abuse left her somewhat unpredictable. Between Erik and me, with help from Estefan, she was much improved. Nevertheless, she was still spooky. When a duck burst off the stream, feathers rattling, Angel reared and I slid off. My ankle twisted when I fell, and it hurt too much to stand.

Thank god I was wearing breeches and boots, I thought. How much worse might it have been?

I made another abortive effort to stand. Surely I could walk the distance to the house; I had done so many times.

No, I couldn't. I sat down again, miserable. I watched Angel's departing hindquarters as she headed for the barn, disregarding my calls and whistles.

As though you could have re-mounted, I mocked myself.

Crawling seemed to be my only option to get home; this would not be pleasant. I prepared to make my slow and painful way back home.

"Claire?" The voice was coming closer. 'Claire?"

"Here!" I responded with relief.

Estefan rode into view on his sturdy little horse. His long limbs almost looked out of place; he swung off the broad, bare back and knelt next to me. His hair was loose and shone as black as Erik's. He dropped Lladro's reins and the horse stayed put.

"We need to teach that to Angel," I groaned, trying to stand again.

"That one!" Estefan rolled his eyes. "She will always be what she is. I saw her run to the barn, reins flapping, and rode this way to look for you."

I tried once more to rise from the ground.

"Don't be stubborn, mi phen. Put your arms around my neck."

I did so, and he lifted me easily. Lladro stood patiently while Estefan settled me on his back. I made to cast a leg over and sit astride but Estefan stopped me.

"I will not let you fall, and neither will Lladro. It will be easier for me to help you down this way."

So it was that we made our slow way back to the house, Estefan with one arm around my waist and me with my fingers entwined in Lladro's mane.

Estefan helped me down and got me settled inside on a divan. He went out to the barn, removed Angel's bridle, and turned her out in the pasture with Lladro.

"Teach that one some manners," I heard him call.

When Estefan returned, he unlaced my boots and tugged them off.

"Your breeches, mi phen," he said. "Those off too, and your stockings."

My years in the theatre had left me with little shame, but I was keenly aware of Erik's handsome half-brother. Heat rose in my face as I managed to shrug out of the trousers without leaving my seat.

Estefan rolled down my stockings in a manner that reminded me far too much of Erik's and my first night together when he'd humbly kissed my feet. Estefan was, however, all business as he examined my ankle.

"Bruised, but not broken," he pronounced.

"You must have a care, mi phen," he added, looking at the slight rounding of my belly. Erik's prediction had come true; I was with child. "No more riding out bareback. Stirrups would have kept you seated."

When Erik and Ornella returned, I expected an angry outburst over my half-dressed state. Instead, Erik took Estefan's part and proclaimed that I must remain quietly occupied indoors until the swelling in my ankle went down. He overrode Estefan's statement that riding with the saddle would be safe.

"No. You will not take that risk again." His tone brooked no resistance.

Erik wrapped my foot and ankle in clean, cotton cloth; Estefan cut a sturdy forked branch to serve as a crutch.

"Nothing will heal this but time, mi phen. And you must be careful of the young one."

I chafed at my confinement, of course. I compromised by crutching out to the pasture to watch Estefan work the horses. He carried a chair out for my use, loading it with so many cushions that I was surprised there was room left for me.

Estefan was a wonder to watch; he started each horse on the long line, warming them up. Even my Josephine, with her damaged wind and scarred knees, was put through her paces and thrived.

When he worked the horses at liberty, I was enthralled. Always starting with his sturdy, spotted gelding, Lladro, he would whistle or use hand signals to cue the horse. Lladro would pivot so closely that it was like one hoof was rooted to the ground. Hotspur, Cesare and Angel learned the signals with patience. Josephine, though, would imitate Lladro as he went through his paces. This was work she knew well and remembered.

VIII

When Erik made a decision, it was law. We usually took precautions against pregnancy throughout our marriage. He feared that, with no one to care for, I would lapse into melancholy as I had done in London. That was his motivation to see me delivered of a child, far more-so than any wish to leave a human legacy.

Pregnancy was an unpleasant experience for me; I wondered why any woman would willingly undergo it a second time. The first three months were a hellish round of nausea and stomach pain that never stopped. Only Ornella's herbal tinctures helped keep my food down. My sprained ankle did nothing to improve my temper.

Erik made no secret of his delight at my pregnancy. For my part, I was miserable. Smells that I had previously loved nauseated me. I felt ungainly as my body changed shape, and exhausted as the being within me drew sustenance from my very bones.

I kept active on the mas to the extent that the men allowed, most often working in the garden. Estefan insisted upon taking over the heavier chores, such as mucking the stalls or feeding the horses.

"It is not right, mi phen," he said. "Let a man do such work."

Ornella similarly took over in the kitchen, because cooking smells were enough to send my gut cramping. Our table never lacked variety, and I came to enjoy the exotic stews and soups that she prepared. I learned some of her recipes; the vegetable ratatouille she made from our aubergines, tomatoes and courgettes became one of my favorite dishes.

When I reached the point that I could no longer even garden, I was fell into a state of depression. All I could do then was lumber around the house as my husband and our Romany friends insisted upon managing all of the chores.

My breasts and belly were so swollen that my corsets no longer fit, let alone my clothing. Ornella fashioned a cloth sling of sorts to support the weight of both abdomen and bosom, which was a tremendous help. Zareh, upon learning of my pregnancy, sent a number of Persian robes for me; their loose shape was well-suited to my condition and his generosity a godsend. Erik had the dressmaker come around as well; there were several maternity gowns made for me, including an elegant one in a red and gold damask, and special corsets to go under them. Thus, I was properly attired for either home or town.

When we retired for the night, Erik would caress my protruding abdomen gently and sometimes drop a warm kiss there. Most nights, he rubbed my belly with perfumed oils, helping my skin as it stretched more than I imagined possible. That Erik found my bloated form appealing surprised me, but we made love regularly nonetheless, becoming very creative indeed.

Illness or no, I found him just as captivating as the day we met. That night of the pachiv was a rebirth for both of us.

IX

I was curled up with my cat, Pierre, when my labor pains began in earnest, although I'd had some back pain for the previous few days. Erik and Ornella had gone into town and I was alone in the house. Estefan was in the barn.

I heaved myself up from the bed, the cat complaining loudly, and went outside. I walked out to the barn, waiting for yet another agonizing cramp to seize me; I knew full well what was happening.

"Estefan?" My trembling voice revealed my fear; I felt wholly unprepared.

I leaned against the doorframe and peered down the barn's wide aisle-way.

"Estefan?" This time a little louder. Why, oh why, was Ornella not at home? I needed her midwifery.

Erik's half-brother looked down from the hayrick and, with an oath, hurried down the ladder.

"Mi phen, we must take you back into the house." He put one strong arm around my waist and walked me back. *"I wish my aunt were here, but we will make do."*

Another cramp, and I cried out.

"Estefan, please. Take Angel and ride to town. She is the fastest. Find them. There is time."

I sank into my favorite chair.

"Please," I begged. "I need Erik." Even as I said the words, I recognized the truth of them. Far more than the midwife, I wanted -- needed -- my husband.

Estefan nodded his assent and left me; very shortly, I heard Angel's hooves on the pathway. I later learned that Estefan attached a lead to her head collar, vaulted onto her bare back and galloped the hearty little mare into town.

I periodically rose from the chair and paced the floor, never straying far from some piece of furniture that I could grasp during one of the godawful contractions. It was all I could do to remain upright when they struck, and I moaned in pain with each one.

When I heard hooves and carriage wheels, I was not at all surprised that Erik was the first one through the door.

"My treasure," he smiled, "I am so excited. You will be fine."

If only I shared his confidence.

"I just want to lie down," I moaned, even though Ornella had told me I must not.

That lady followed shortly, carrying oil cloth and a most unusual piece of furniture: a low stool with a curved section cut out.

"Come into the bedroom," she said, leading the way. Erik and Estefan supported me on either side.

Ornella situated me on the stool, explaining that I would have an easier time of delivery than "the gadja who lie in bed."

"This will be messy and unpleasant," she went on. "Make no mistake. But you will indeed be fine and so will the young one."

Another contraction gripped me as Ornella sent Erik and Estefan out of the room.

"This is women's work, the magic of bringing life into the world."

She unhooked my robe, pulled it off over my head, and unwound the support garments.

"Now, my sister, grip my hand when the pain comes and we will do this together."

Ornella massaged my belly with some of the same oils that Erik had used. The aromas of sandalwood, oranges and cinnamon filled the room; she pushed down on the top of my abdomen whenever I squeezed her hand.

It seemed like forever; I lost all sense of time and could think of nothing but the pain. Ornella would periodically tell me to push again with her; I just wanted it to be over.

And then, it was, with just one more mighty contraction that brought a scream of pain from me; I felt as though I was being rent limb from limb. Amid the mess of blood and placenta on the oilcloth, Ornella tied off an umbilicus and handed my squalling daughter to me.

"Give her to suckle," Ornella directed, and the infant latched on to a nipple with minimal encouragement.

She had black hair, but I knew that it might just as easily fall out and come in a different color. Likewise, I knew her eyes might not remain blue. Her long, slender fingers, more than anything else, marked her as Erik's daughter.

Ornella cleaned up around me and then took the child to wash her. Once she was clean, swaddled and diapered, Ornella directed her attention to me.

"Stand if you can and I'll wash you up." She briskly sponged me off from the ewer and pitcher nearby.

Then, just as though I had my monthly, she folded clean flannel sheeting into a pad and belted it around me. Next she helped me into my bloomers.

"You'll be sore and bleeding for a while yet. Now, arms up."

She slipped a clean night rail over my head.

"In bed with you," she commanded, and then sat next to me. She unpinned my hair and brushed it out loose over my shoulders. Then she put the sleeping infant in my arms.

"Now, my sister,' she smiled conspiratorially, "Watch as your husband falls in love with you yet again."

From the pages of Erik's journal

When Ornella finally let me in the room, I pushed past her without so much as a by-your-leave. Estefan had restrained me at every cry, most particularly the last and loudest, to keep me in the parlor and away from the birth. Every agonized sound Claire made cut through me like the sharpest blade.

"You don't understand," I insisted. "She needs me."

"And this, my brother, is woman's magic. Soon enough you will go to her."

I relented, but only reluctantly. Now, I would see my wife and no one would gainsay me.

Claire's eyes were smudged and tired, but she was radiant. Her hair streamed down her back as she sat, propped up by numerous pillows, holding the child.

My child.

Ornella left us alone, taking a wad of bloodied cloth and the birthing stool with her. I sat down on the bed.

"My treasure," I kissed her forehead. "How are you?"

"Exhausted."

"May I?" I gestured toward the babe, and Claire placed the infant in my hands.

"Your daughter," she whispered.

"My dreams fulfilled," I replied. "A wife, a child ... to me, these are my victory."

"What would you name your daughter, my husband?"

I paused only briefly. "Veronique."

Yes, Veronique, from the Greek bere nike -- bringing victory.

That baby is Mommy, Clarice thought as she closed the book and flopped back on her pillows. Lucifer meowed in protest, stretched and moved to the foot of the bed for a bath.

And how direct *Grand-mère* was about childbirth. No one talked about such things so frankly, in Clarice's experience. She had always assumed, vaguely, that she would have children one day -- without the slightest idea what pregnancy would be like. She knew where children came from, of course, but having children was always talked about with such reverence by Mommy's friends ... as well as in a speculative but delighted way by Clarice's friends, that she had never imagined it being a hardship. What would it be like to be unable to do the things that you really loved because a baby was growing inside you? She'd never given it a thought.

Grand-mère had not found it miraculous at all, that much was clear. Clarice thought it sounded perfectly dreadful.

She went back to her reading.

X

While Erik delighted in being a father, my own enthusiasm for child-rearing was not what it could have been. I cried just as easily as the baby, and I was tired all of the time. Sometimes I would find myself staring at her and wondering what on earth Erik had been thinking -- or, for that matter, what had made me consent. I had never particularly wanted a child, but I was so caught up in his desire for fatherhood that I dismissed my own misgivings.

We were neither of us youngsters, and to change our ordered existence, so hard-won, in this way? Madness.

Ornella insisted that I spend some time outdoors each day and pushed me to eat more ("the babes take it all from you elsewise").

I also felt peculiar about nursing. I was, of course, aware that it was a natural act. Yet, I felt so detached from Veronique that I had to force myself to do it at times. Add to that the way I had loved for Erik to kiss my breasts during lovemaking and the peculiar sensation of desire that came with feeding a child from them disturbed me.

I knew that melancholia was creeping up on me again in the wake of Veronique's birth; by now I knew the signs as clearly as I knew my face in the mirror. Surely this should have been a tremendously happy time for me? Was this not what I had been reared for: to give a child, an heir, to my husband? To ensure that the family name carried on?

Then why did I just want to run away?

Erik did what he could; diapering, bathing and the like were no problem for him. When Veronique cried in hunger he would bring her to me and watch with unconcealed admiration even as I was listless in nursing.

Ornella watched this quietly for a few weeks and then sat me down for a talking-to.

"My sister," she said quietly, "You are not alone. Many women do not delight in their children at first. I have seen it and marked it well."

"But why? I would do anything for Erik, and yet I am not happy to be the mother of his child. And I am so very tired of nursing."

She sighed. "I know. Yet, you must carry on for a time. None here know how to keep a cow, and for you to safely stop feeding the milk must always be from the same animal."

She was right, of course; it was common knowledge that milk had to come from the same cow every time, should bottle feeding be necessary, in order for an infant to thrive.

I wanted to weep at what felt like a ridiculous burden. I knew it was illogical to feel that way, of course, but that was the truth of it. I think that, more than anything else, I resented sharing Erik with his own daughter. Again, a sensation with no basis in logic, but present nonetheless.

For example, I would never forget the night I taught Erik to waltz. It was one of the few things he could not teach himself; there were limits to his genius in that regard.

We stood in the foyer of the Place des Vosges townhouse, the entryway carpet rolled back to reveal a gleaming hardwood floor. With the toe of my slipper indicating one of the boards, I said "This is our center."

Then, I showed him the "right-two-three, left-pivot" rhythm of the steps and we practiced together.

"Now," I said, "put your right hand flat against my back, just below the left shoulder blade and take my right hand in your left."

He did so, and I placed my left hand on his right arm, just below the shoulder.

"Now, start with the left pivot step; I will be doing the right-two-three."

There were some mis-steps before Erik's natural musician's grace took over. Before long, we were waltzing around the foyer as though Erik had been dancing forever.

When we stopped, we looked into one another's eyes for what seemed like eternity before he lowered his sinfully beautiful mouth to mine. Not long thereafter, we were upstairs in my bed, limbs entwined in passionate lovemaking.

Our days of dancing together had ended, but whenever his health allowed, Erik would pick up his daughter and waltz her around the room. The smile on his face and her child's laughter were a balm to all of our souls under the circumstances.

Clarice loved to dance; she could envision *Grand-mère* and Erik dancing in the hallway, just as she had written. Scooping up a protesting Lucifer into her arms, she practiced the waltz just as Claire had described it. She no longer envisioned Jimmy Aaron as her partner; now it was a faceless someone whom she pretended led her through the dance: a faceless someone with pale blue eyes.

With a smile, she put her cat down and got ready for bed. Perhaps she would dream of love.

Chapter 9

The following Saturday, Clarice made her way to Golden Gate Park. She'd taken her voice lesson that morning, and from there took the bus to the Polo Field. Her face was flushed and happy; the lesson had been splendid. She'd been given an art song to prepare for the winter recital: Charles Gounod's "Ave Maria." It was one of her favorite pieces, and she was very excited. In fact, she found herself telling Billy all about it.

"Do say you'll come and hear me sing," she said, shocked at her own boldness.

"I would be honored," he replied. "You just let me know when and where. I'll be there."

He gave her a leg up into the saddle and they took off at a gentle lope. Clarice had not really noticed how pleasant his face was before.

Billy, for his part, found himself telling her about his studies at college; he wanted to be a newspaper reporter, but there was just no money for school. So, he had turned his hobby of horseback riding into a job, teaching others how to feel at home and safe in the saddle. He found Clarice easy to talk to, and she certainly was easy to look at, with her wavy auburn hair and green eyes. She rode well, too.

Very easy to look at indeed, like a movie star, he thought.

That night, Clarice opened *Grand-mère*'s journal and read some more before bedtime.

XI

In time, my body healed from the physical rigors of childbearing and Erik and I were able to make love again. The physical tenderness between us did much to heal my mind and before long the melancholy was back on the shelf where it belonged.

That is not to say that all was perfect or easy. On one particularly difficult night, Veronique lay shrieking in her cradle. I had fed her, rocked her ... nothing helped. I wept with frustration; nothing I offered would comfort her. Erik eventually stalked out of the room scowling, returning with his violin. He tucked the instrument under his chin and played Brahms' "Lullaby" while standing over her-- and she fell silent as Erik's music wove its spell. Eventually she slept.

From then on, Erik would play or sing her to sleep. Before long, she slept through the night and I, too, was able to rest again.

When Veronique was nearly a year old, Ornella and Estefan came again. Estefan decided that Veronique must know about horses and would hold her in front of him for short rides on Lladro's back. She would giggle and smile for her uncle just as she did her father.

With me she was still diffident, as though unsure of how she would be received. I wondered how much my misery after her birth had really touched her. Surely she could not perceive it at such a young age?

Estefan handed Veronique to Erik, who kissed her little cheek and stroked her black hair. Her eyes were now green, like her father's. She was serious most of the time, but her laughter and smiles for her father and uncle was unreserved.

Veronique was just two years old when Erik ordered the tiny violin from the House of Chanot, the same French violin-makers who created his precious instrument. It was his violin in miniature, with the sloping curves and unusual f-holes. Though Veronique was only just toddling, he was convinced that she was ready to learn the basics. He showed her how to properly hold the instrument under her chin, and taught her to play a simple Mozart tune pizzicato style.

"Time enough for bowing," he said. "For now, we will work on fingering."

As sure as night followed day, he was right. Veronique took to the violin like a fish to water; by the time she was three years old, she was bowing. She and Erik played simple etude duets together every day. His pride in her musicianship was palpable. To my surprise, my temperamental husband proved an able and patient teacher. Veronique adored him.

XII

Estefan and Ornella stayed with us during the last few weeks of Erik's life. Ornella was a great help with Veronique, who was nearly four years old.

Ornella, Veronique and I had just come in from the garden when Estefan came out of the bedroom. I had surrendered it to Erik as his cough worsened; he insisted that we sleep apart so that he did not disturb me. He was often so weak that leaving the bed for the water closet left him exhausted Likewise, he could no longer sing or play the violin.

Estefan carried Erik's shaving kit and a bag. His expression was solemn.

"He insisted," he shrugged in response to my questioning look. He opened the bag to show me the black hair he had clipped from Erik's scalp. "He said it was just too hot and uncomfortable."

I went into the bedroom where Erik was still seated, shirtless, on a stool. He had long since stopped wearing his mask because it was uncomfortable when he coughed; his hairpiece and the now-shorn raven locks had been his last vanity.

"What do you think of my haircut, Claire," he sighed as I caressed the cropped stubble.

"I think you look like a prisoner."

"My love, I think that soon you and I shall both be free."

I held his face to my bosom as we both sobbed.

Later that night, Estefan handed me a piece of russet silk cut from the end of the sash Erik wore the night Veronique was conceived. Carefully wrapped inside it was one lock of jet black hair, still redolent with Erik's sandalwood soap. I put it in on the top shelf of the armoire, to be kept always; Estefan understood all too well.

On the last night, Erik asked me to keep him company. His eyes were glassy and he was feverish. He'd refused to eat even a simple blancmange for the past few days, sipping at water or tea.

Ornella and Estefan took Veronique to spend the night in the vardo; we all sensed what was to come.

I crawled into bed next to Erik, who leaned his ruined right cheek against my bosom. I stroked his cropped hair gently.

"I love the sound of your heart, Claire." His voice was gravelly, as though the cough that stole his musical tenor would not be satisfied until his speech was destroyed too.

"Will you read to me," he asked. "There is a book of poetry on the nightstand."

It was the little volume of sonnets that he had read to me during our honeymoon.

"Of course I will," I said. I got up, adjusted the lamp wick and opened the book to the page he had marked.

I got back into bed and adjusted the botis quilts around the two of us. I started reading with "My mistress' eyes are nothing like the sun" and didn't stop until Erik's labored breathing eased in sleep.

I put the book aside and watched him as he slept. I knew just what sort of vigil I kept.

I lost track of time, but it was well past midnight when Erik woke in a horrible paroxysm of coughing. He spat blood over and over again into a kerchief.

"My treasure," he whispered as he looked up at me and grasped my hand. "I will always love you."

"I love you, Erik." Tears streamed down my cheeks, but he smiled and closed his eyes. I kissed him gently and he sighed.

Moments later, he was gone. I sat with him for a few minutes before I picked up the lamp and went out to the vardo. There, no words were necessary. Ornella tucked me into her bed and went into the house to prepare Erik for the undertaker.

As always, Erik had planned carefully. The cemetery and burial had been arranged for some time. It was the work of minutes for Estefan to drive me into town and see the priest. He sent the horse-drawn hearse and coffin back to the house with us.

Ornella had been busy in the kitchen, not only cooking food but boiling a couple of my dresses and Veronique's frocks in black dye.

"I know, my sister, that you do not hold with this custom," she said as Estefan and the priest went into the bedroom. "Still, you will need these things."

I nodded and followed the men into the room. Erik was laid out in his elegant evening attire, hands crossed on his chest with the left on top to show his wedding ring. Ornella had clipped his hairpiece to fit in with the rest of his shorn hair, and it put it in place along with his mask.

"Mi phen," Estefan put an arm protectively around my waist. "Do you need more time?"

Of course I needed more time. How would I bring up Veronique alone? Care for the mas?

I did not give voice to my racing thoughts. Instead, I bent forward to kiss Erik's lips one last time. They were cool to the touch now, where they had been warm and sensually yielding in life.

I straightened then and squared my shoulders.

"Maman?" Veronique stood in the doorway, holding Ornella's hand.

"She wants to say goodbye, too," the older woman explained.

I nodded and the two of them came in. Ornella whispered something to Veronique, who nodded and then kissed her father's cheek.

"Tante Ornella says Papa's soul is with the angels now, and that I must be a good, big girl for you."

I burst into tears then and Ornella led me out of the room, holding my hand just as she did Veronique's, so that Estefan and the priest could move Erik's body to the hearse outside.

XIII

It was fortunate that Ornella had prepared so much food, for the melancholia was very much upon me after Erik's death. I went through the motions of my life only because of Veronique. Had it not been for Erik's daughter, I doubt I would have survived.

As always, Erik had known me better than I knew myself. The useful work of looking after our child turned my focus outward of necessity; melancholia could only take hold when I focused inward.

Shortly after Erik's funeral, I found Estefan burning a pair of leather trousers and a white shirt. When a familiar silk sash was about to join the pyre, I asked why.

"If he'd had his own vardo, I would burn that," he explained. "It's sending his things to the next world in smoke. He lived among the Rom, and we share a father, Claire. How could I not honor his passing as the Romany do?"

"He wanted Veronique to have his violin when she is older," I said.

"He told me so," Estefan replied. "I don't think I could have brought myself to put it in the fire anyway." He wiped at his eyes then, and insisted it was because of the smoke.

Ornella came to tell me that she and Estefan were moving on, and that she doubted we would meet again.

"My sister, never doubt that you will find us if you are in need," she said, "But you will one day be far from these shores."

"No," I replied. "This is the home that Erik and I made together. I will bide here."

I would later remember her amused smile and nod as we said our farewells.

"Ashen devele, Romele." May you go with God.

I waved good-bye until the vardo was out of sight. I didn't know what would happen next, but I had to find strength to carry on ... strength enough for me, and for our daughter.

Clarice closed the journal and reached for the violet-embroidered handkerchief she kept under her pillow. She was weeping unabashedly. Claire had written so vividly about Erik's death that she felt like a witness to the entire thing. Mommy had been a brave little girl, that was for sure.

After drying her eyes, Clarice went downstairs to supper. She hugged Veronique tightly and, when asked what that was for, said "Because I felt like it."

"That was a first," Daddy said before bowing his head to bless the food.

The week passed quickly, between singing lessons, riding lessons and school. Billy Wakefield had not made good on his promise to come calling, but they spent time together during

Clarice's riding lessons. He was so busy with work and college, he explained, that it just seemed like there was no time.

"I want to take you out for a proper dinner date," he said. "Be thinking of a restaurant you like, so that we can plan for it. I promise I'll do it."

Clarice told him all about Sam Wo's, and Billy said that he thought Chinatown would be good fun. She thought about mentioning the Winter Ball, but didn't think that Billy would care to come to a high school dance. The restaurant was a better idea.

"You can show me around," he said.

That day, after the lesson, he kissed Clarice on the cheek before she left. Since that first bold kiss, he'd been absolutely circumspect. This was only the second time he'd kissed her, and her cheek felt like it was on fire. Her tummy felt funny when she got in the car. Mommy took one look at her face, smiled knowingly, and didn't say a thing.

That night, Clarice picked up Claire's journal again.

XIV

 I could never have predicted what happened next: about a year after Erik passed away, Gilbert Rochambeau came calling. Like me, he was widowed. He had always been a dear friend, and he had kissed me once on a night when Erik took way more opium than he should have done. Gilbert was mortified at his own boldness, and I feared that my violent husband would do him harm. In a manner of speaking, he did: he humiliated both of us and refused to accept Gilbert's resignation as my majordomo. He wanted Gilbert to be keenly aware of his folly.

 It must be said once again that Erik was not always a kind man.

 Gilbert's and my courtship and eventual marriage were the talk of Avignon. I was a wealthy widow and many of the Provençal men, even from as far away as Aix, had tried to court me to no avail. Every trufficulteur, bourgeois, widower and youth, or so it felt, came calling with a desire to meet the Widow LeMaître and perhaps marry into controlling the fortune left by her mysterious, ailing husband.

 I did not leave home unless Veronique and I were both dressed in mourning weeds, although I loathed the custom. I called the plain black clothes "my armor." Ornella was correct when she said we would welcome the protection that mourning gave us. In public, at least, the men of our region would behave in a circumspect fashion as they greeted us on the street.

I was tired and seldom smiled toward the end of Erik's illness and after his death. I had become a very serious woman, watching my beloved husband waste away. I seldom laughed, and could only be described as careworn.

I sometimes think that the men who tried to court me counted on that to get closer to me; they didn't care whether or not I smiled as long as they could perhaps marry me and obtain the property Erik bequeathed me. More precious than all of that were the bankbook and passport in my own name that Erik arranged before his death; those could be revoked by a less understanding husband. Coverture was still the law of the land, and men benefitted mightily from it. I had long since reached the point where fortune hunters exhausted me and I didn't care if I never had a gentleman in my life again.

Until the day that Gilbert came up the garden path, road dust marring his clothes; he had walked from the train station. That was the day that the roses began to bloom in my cheeks again. As I said, Erik had been gone for nearly a year by then.

Veronique wrinkled up her nose when she saw him; even during his illness Erik was fastidious about his clothes, and she believed that was how gentlemen should look. I was so excited to see him, though, that I did not care how dusty and road-sore he looked. When he confessed his long-standing love for me and gave me a gentle kiss in the arbor, he reawakened many a long-suppressed desire.

I brought Gilbert into the house for our afternoon tea and introduced him to Veronique. She had quietly laid another place at our simple table, and behaved herself admirably. After tea, she played her violin for Gilbert. He was very polite in his praise of her etude, observing that she had inherited Erik's talents.

Gilbert stayed for supper that evening as well. After the meal, I bade Veronique get ready for bed. When she came back to the parlor to say her goodnights, Gilbert was sitting on the divan next to me, brushing my long, thick hair as he had done once before in Paris. Then he had been my majordomo and Erik's valet. Now, things were different. I was seated at an angle so that Gilbert was behind me; my eyes were closed and my head tilted toward him. I felt blissful and relaxed for the first time in many months.

"Goodnight, Maman," Veronique announced loudly.

I opened my heavy, dreamy eyes.

"Goodnight, ma petite. Sleep well. I'll come in just a moment to tuck you in."

She obediently returned to her room, but looked over her shoulder to see Gilbert kiss the nape of my neck. I caressed his cheek as I stood to follow my child.

"I shan't be long, mon vieux," I smiled at him. Nor did I dally.

XV

When I came back to the parlor after settling Veronique in bed, Gilbert stood and took me in his arms. I rested my cheek against his chest, listening to his heartbeat as I relaxed in his embrace.

"I must go," he said, kissing the top of my head. "It's a bit of a walk back to my rooms and I will not put you out by taking one of your horses."

"No," I said, "you need not go." I tilted my chin up to meet his brown eyes. "I don't want you to go, Gilbert."

"Are you sure, Claire?" For a brief moment, I saw again the sad, tired man Gilbert had been in my cousin's employ: the man who believed he had no worth.

I reached up to untie his cravat and opened his collar while I replied.

"Monsieur Rochambeau, are you questioning my judgment?"

"No, Madame LeMaître," he whispered as he shrugged out of his chocolate brown suit coat. "My lady's wish is my command."

"Mmm," I sighed as I unbuttoned his dark green waistcoat. "Is that how it's to be, then?"

His smile was both shy and sensual, almost boyish.

"How may I serve madame," he murmured, leaning forward to graze my brow with his lips. "I am yours to direct."

He entwined his fingers in my hair and brought his lips to mine. His tongue slid into my mouth, his kiss passionate and tender at the same time. I returned his kiss with a hunger born of long chastity; my ardor surprised me, for I had thought that part of my life to be over.

"Monsieur Rochambeau," I sighed when we separated, "I suggest we repair to the boudoir."

He lifted my hand to his lips and gently kissed my palm.

"But of course, madame."

Without the walking stick I had bought for him in London, Gilbert's steps were still somewhat halting. He sat down on the bedstead and removed his shoes; one of them had a built-up sole to compensate for the badly-set break of his youth.

I seated myself at the vanity and began to braid my hair.

"No, Claire, please," Gilbert said. "Leave it loose for me."

I turned around on the little stool.

"All right," I smiled as I unbuttoned the bodice of my calico frock. I stood up, stepped out of the dress, and slipped out of my espadrilles.

"So beautiful," Gilbert sighed as he removed his shirt and waistcoat. "But so thin, mon amour. Your waist is even smaller than I remembered."

I stood before him in my pantaloons, chemise and corset, and he put his hands on my waist.

"I think, monsieur, that now is not the time for concerns about my dietary habits."

In all the time that Gilbert was my majordomo, I had never seen him without a shirt. His arms were well-muscled. Like Erik, he wore no singlet beneath his shirt; his chest was likewise muscular, his abdomen flat and trim with a tracery of dark gold hair emphasizing his build.

I curled my fingers through Gilbert's hair and kissed him again. How different his kisses were from Erik's, and not just because of his beard and mustache. Erik had been sure of himself, masterful. Gilbert's kisses were loving and gentle, but shy. It was a very different experience for me; I felt as though I were being savored like a fine wine.

As we kissed again, Gilbert reached behind me to loosen my stays. He eased the ribbons out slowly, stopping now and then to allow my blood to circulate. To undo a corset too quickly was to invite a fainting spell. When the ribbons were loose enough, he unhooked my busk and let the corset fall away. He lowered his mouth to my bosom, teasing the buds of my nipples through the sheer linen chemise.

"*Oh, god,*" *I moaned quietly. His very touch made me burn; the flames of desire had been banked for far too long. I raked his shoulders with my nails.*

"*Ma cherie,*" *he sighed, "if only you knew how long I have dreamed of this."*

I unbuttoned my chemise and untied the ribbons of my pantaloons, discarding the last of my garments. Gilbert pulled me closer to him again, cupping my bottom in his hands.

"*What may I do to please my lady?" His voice was husky and thick with desire.*

"Ah, my handsome majordomo," I teased. "You are wearing far too many clothes."

He stood up and unbuttoned his trousers, dropping them to the floor, and removed his socks.

He was much the same height as Erik had been, nearly a foot taller than me. He was, however, self-conscious about his nudity where Erik had bordered on insolent, as though daring me to look at him.

I stepped over to the bedside lamp and turned up the wick so that the golden glow shown brighter on him.

"Never be ashamed, Gilbert. You are so handsome, and your body is beautiful to me."

"Do you think so, really?" His eyes were soft with emotion.

"Please lie down. You have nothing to fear with me."

Gilbert returned to the plain iron bedstead and settled atop the colorful boutis quilt. I laid down next to him and kissed him gently.

"So shy of me, suddenly?" I asked softly. "Why is that?"

"I do not know, Claire. As I said, I have thought of being with you so many times over the years. And now, I ..." His voice trailed off.

"Perhaps you are afraid that you disappoint?"

He nodded. "You have never seen ... all of me ... before."

"Mm-hmm." I deliberately caressed the knotted scar on his leg; he winced, but not from pain. "Did you think that this would horrify me Gilbert? After my poor Philippe's burns? And Erik? After my friendship with poor Joseph Merrick? Oh no, mon vieux. You do not disappoint at all."

I trailed my fingers lightly up his thigh. He closed his eyes and relaxed against the pillows, shivering a bit at my caress.

"Surely, my dear one, you are accustomed to a woman's touch?"

"Not like this. Honor was one for total darkness in the room and lifting her night rail, poor girl. Otherwise, it's been only brief couplings with whores."

He groaned as I moved my hand from his thigh to his manhood, stroking him gently.

"I am no frightened virgin, Gilbert, and I am no fallen woman gone to the bad and in a hurry. I want to get to know your body, all of it. You asked what would please me; right now, let me pleasure you."

I moved astride him and leaned forward for another kiss; Gilbert caught my hair and entwined his fingers in its dark length, pulling me even closer.

"I had no idea you were such a vixen," *he moaned as I rocked my hips against his hardness, letting him feel the heat from my body.*

"Do you feel my desire for you," *I whispered, my breath warm on his ear.*

I trailed kisses down his chest and belly, tickling his navel with my tongue while he continued caressing my hair. When I gently set my tongue to his manhood, he cried out.

"Dear god, Claire. No one has ever ..."

"Mmm, cheri ... then let me."

I licked and teased him for a few minutes, feeling his tumescence increase. I stroked the cool weight of his testes while he moaned in delight. I could tell that he was nigh unto release, but I wanted him to wait. I moved back up to kiss his lips again.

"Dear lady, I beg you," he groaned into my ear. He slid his mouth down to the base of my throat, his closely trimmed beard and mustache grazing the delicate skin there. I would surely have a lover's rash the next day, but I was far from caring.

I laid down, fanning my hair out over the pillows and Gilbert moved to join me. He slipped gently between my knees and I guided his velvety hardness toward my waiting mound.

"Tomorrow, my dearest," I whispered, "I will see those whiskers gone."

"Anything," he groaned as he entered me for the first time. "Anything for you."

Gilbert's lovemaking was simple and tender; he whispered endearments as he moved deeper within me, and cried out my name when he reached his climax. I held him as he fell asleep, my fingers entwined in his dark golden hair. While I could not help remembering Erik's passionate and varied ways in the boudoir, I also knew that Gilbert would indeed do anything to please me.

Clarice was blushing as she turned out the light. That her grandmother had been so bold with her lover no longer shocked her, although her frank writings gave Clarice some unexpected feelings. She found herself thinking about Billy Wakefield's kiss as she drifted off to sleep.

The next day seemed interminable; all she wanted to do was go home to read more of her grandmother's diary. But there were classes to get through first. When she saw Jimmy Aaron in the hallway with Eleanor Fountain, she was surprised to notice that she felt ... nothing.

At long last, supper was over and chores done. Clarice ran upstairs, Lucifer at her heels, and picked up Claire's journal again.

XVI

The next morning, I made good on my promise before I would even consider breakfast; Gilbert's beard simply had to go. I seated him at the kitchen table while I stropped Erik's razor. Gilbert's shirt was open and his sleeves rolled to the elbow; he was the picture of sated relaxation. I wore a simple skirt and blouse with a Provençal print apron of red and gold over the top. My hair hung loose down my back, held away from my face with tortoiseshell combs Erik had given me years before. I felt young and happy, as though a tremendous burden had been lifted from me with Gilbert's presence.

"I have never liked chin whiskers on a man, cheri," I said. "So, now I will be your valet and shave you."

"As my mistress commands," he laughed. "Let me pay the barber with a kiss."

I leaned forward to do just that. "And now, mon vieux, I will see that face of yours again. Adieu, barbe et moustache."

I shaved Erik many times while he was ill, and had become most efficient. I poured some warm water from the tea kettle into a bowl and added some cool water from the pump; next I dipped Erik's shaving brush into the bowl and then into the soap. I stroked the lather onto Gilbert's face, stopping to kiss him once more and laughing as I got soap on my face. I wiped it away with my apron hem.

Gilbert noticed Veronique standing in the kitchen doorway, solemnly observing the proceedings.

"Bonjour, ma petite," he said to her. "Are you come to watch your mama change my face?"

She shook her head. "I came to have breakfast."

I stroked the soap and whiskers away from Gilbert's face, rinsing the shining blade as I went..

"We shall break our fast as soon as I have finished revealing Gilbert's handsome face again," I smiled. Many more kisses "paid the barber" by the time I was finished.

After tidying up the shaving things, I prepared omelets for all of us to share. I was glad that Ornella had helped me become more proficient in the kitchen. Veronique kept cutting her eyes at Gilbert in a manner that I would have found disapproving in an adult, let alone my own child. It was not a comfortable meal.

After breakfast, Gilbert insisted upon returning to his rooms in town. I loaned Angel to him; she was a delight to ride after Estefan's work, with a surprisingly soft mouth and a light step. She nickered whenever she saw me, and had delightful ground manners that made her easy to saddle, groom and mount. I told Gilbert he could use her for as long as he liked; Josephine, Cesare and Hotspur were all taller and more difficult for him because of his leg.

I was sad to see him go back to town so soon, but was still warm with the delight of our lovemaking. The years had fallen away so quickly when I was in his arms; I was able to forget my cares for a time.

I washed the breakfast dishes, and then read for a while to Veronique. When she professed a desire to nap, I agreed.

"I will be in the arbor reading, ma petite," I said. "Please come and get me when you are up and we will have our luncheon."

I tucked her in again; it was unusual for her to sleep again so early in the day, but we had found ourselves in an unusual state of excitement.

I took my hairbrush and my book with me to the arbor; in the event that I chose to nap, I would want to tidy myself far better than I had yesterday. I plaited my hair into a long braid, took off my shoes and stockings, and tucked my bare feet up under my skirt on the chaise longue. I enjoyed the warmth of the morning sun but had a care to stay in the shade lest I turn brown as a berry.

It was well that I had anticipated a nap, for I did indeed fall asleep. It was nearing noon when I awoke. Veronique could be heard playing with the cats not far away; she had chosen not to wake me when she could have a game with Pierre and Elise.

I stretched a bit and then undid my braid. I was brushing my hair when Gilbert rode up again.

"No, don't stop," he said as he dismounted. He took a box out of the saddle bag that hung over Angel's withers. "I would love to paint you like that."

"Whilst brushing my hair?" I responded.

"Just so." *He pulled a small canvas on a stretcher from the box, which turned out to contain paints and have a palette tucked in the lid. "I had thought to do a scene of this arbor, but you have inspired me to do something else again."*

He removed his hat and jacket, and rolled up his shirtsleeves. He studied the scene from various angles and stroked his newly-bared chin..

"I wonder, cherie, if you would consider undressing? I have an idea."

"What on earth, Gilbert?" I trusted him completely but was puzzled.

"I will pose you, Claire. Nothing ... untoward ... will show."

I sent Veronique into the house to practice her violin; I had not reared her to be shy of human bodies, but I did not need for her to see me posing either. I did not want to explain myself to the mamans in town if she should say something.

I disrobed and Gilbert arranged me on the chaise. He posed me in a three-quarters' view, facing away from him, my hair down my back. I held my brush as though in mid-stroke on a thick lock that draped over my shoulder and covered my bosom. He sketched quickly with a charcoal pencil. and then mixed some paints on the palette. I could not see what he was doing very well, even though I cut my eyes at him several times. He painted for a good while, even though the canvas was small. I considered myself fortunate that this was not a life-sized portrait as hung in some homes, as he soon gave me leave to dress again.

When I stepped around to look at what he had done, the image was stunning. He had captured the entire scene perfectly, but the colors were not at all as nature had made them. My hair was a shade of blue tinged with yellow and red where the sunlight touched it, my body a pale pink-toned ivory. The flowers around me were a riot of color, far brighter than nature made them, and the brightly colored boutis that covered the cushions of my chaise was recreated in softer hues. The effect was unusual, striking, and a delight to the eye. The pose, despite my nudity, was as tasteful as any Titian.

"There is a man in Paris called Gustave Moreau, and another called Henri Matisse who have started using color in this style," Gilbert explained as he cleaned his brushes. "I have wanted to try it for some time."

"It is a beautiful piece, Gilbert. I have never seen its like."

I was surprised at how much I liked Gilbert's unconventional painting. Because it would need some time to dry, we propped the canvas on the parlor mantelpiece. It grew on me more with each passing day.

Veronique, from whom I had anticipated some uncomfortable questions, merely remarked that Maman's hair was not that color -- but that it would be beautiful if it were.

I invited Gilbert to stay to supper again; likewise, he shared our breakfast. Waking to his kiss and caresses was a pleasure in and of itself, but to have someone with whom I could talk about days gone by was a special delight. I had come to believe that a respectful, gentle lover was unlikely; Gilbert's return was a small miracle.

XVII

Gilbert rode back and forth between the boarding house and our farm several times a week. It was not long before the men who had continued their vain attempts to court me ceased their attentions -- to my great relief. "Yon gentleman from Paris," as they referred to Gilbert, had my full attention. It never occurred to them that the man wearing such fine suits hailed from neighboring Camargue. It could only be that the Widow LeMaître's head was turned by yet another artistic Parisian. After all, that had been the case of her late husband. There was vague disapproval, of course; the artist set were considered just slightly above the demi-monde by many.

No matter how much the gossips hid behind their fans when Veronique and I went to the shops in Avignon, I heard their remarks. I cared very little for their opinions, which was no surprise. I had been well-trained in the London drawing rooms, after all; no hateful gossip could offend me anymore.

One night while brushing my hair before bed, Gilbert asked to paint me again -- this time in his rooms. He told me his idea for the portrait, and I agreed. We arranged a day and time; I left Veronique in the care of our neighbor, Madame Robillard, and rode into town on Josephine. I was sedately seated on the side-saddle I seldom used. In the saddlebag were the items Gilbert had asked me to bring.

He met me in the parlor and introduced me to his elderly concierge, Madame Despereau. Madame was, like me, a widow. Renting rooms helped her income, and she was more than happy to turn a blind eye when gentleman boarders had female callers.

Gilbert's room was light-filled and tidy. He had arranged his easel in one corner; a table held paints, brushes, palettes and linseed oil. By this time, the first small canvas was moved from my farmhouse and had been framed, propped against a wall.

"I have an idea to do some studies of you," he explained as his rolled up his shirtsleeves. "I want to show the canvasses to Monsieur Matisse at his atelier in Paris, with a view to studying with him."

I must have looked stricken, for he wrapped his arms around me and kissed the top of my head while tugging the pins out of my hair.

"Not yet, my love, I'm not going anywhere." He ran his fingers through my hair, loosening it over my back and shoulders as he kissed me. It was not lost on me how easily both the endearment and the reassurance came to his lips.

He stepped away from me and picked up the saddlebag I had brought with me. I unbuttoned the snug jacket of my riding habit and disrobed as he overturned the bag on the bed. A long lace shawl and Erik's shaving bag tumbled out, along with my comb and brush. Gilbert tossed my hairpins down next to them.

"Are you sure you're willing to do this?" he asked me, as he had when he first proposed the painting.

"Of course! I think it's a fascinating idea for a portrait."

I sat down at the dresser, facing the mirror. Gilbert draped the shawl so that I was partially covered. He looked into the mirror to see that he was getting the effect he wanted.

He then combed my hair out down my back, separating one long lock over to the front. He kissed my bare shoulder as he returned to the bed, rummaging through Erik's bag until he found the sharp barber's shears.

"In all of my years as a valet, I never cut a lady's hair," he said as he knelt behind me. "And yet, this portrait idea has been in my thoughts every time I recall that night in Paris when you sold your locks to the opera's wig maker."

He inserted the shears into my hair just below my shoulder blades and closed the blades. Chestnut brown tresses fell to the floor as he snipped away, leaving my hair much as I had kept it in my equestrian days -- save for that one lock.

This he had me hold in one hand while I had the shears in the other; I posed as though in mid-cut.

Gilbert went to his easel and drew the scene, much as he had done before. He painted a rear view, my face reflected in the mirror. When he had finished the painting, which was the same size as the last one, he cut the one long lock off to match the others. This time, he saved part of the hair in a handkerchief which he tucked into a drawer as a keepsake.

I donned my camisole and pantaloons and came around to look at the work. Again, his use of color was astonishing. My hair was vermillion red this time, with lights of blue and gold in the brilliant tones. The color was likewise captured in the mass of hair on the floor behind the chair. My reflection showed concentration, as though I really had lopped off my own tresses.

In short, Gilbert had again captured the scene in his own fashion.

I swept up the discarded hair as Gilbert sank onto the bed, rubbing his leg; he had stood for a long while to do the painting. When I had finished the clean-up, I joined him.

He ran his fingers through my shortened locks, caressing the back of my skull as he did so.

"I have never forgotten how proud and beautiful you looked that night," he whispered as I unbuttoned his shirt. "Erik had behaved as though your very hair belonged to him, and so you sold it. When you dropped the money at his feet and went upstairs with those curls just touching your shoulders, I wanted you more than words can say."

"Really," I whispered as I unhooked the braces from his trousers.

"Mmm, yes ..." His whisper was more ragged. "I had a vision of you in front of a mirror, cutting your hair ... just as I painted you. So rebellious ..."

He reclined against the pillows as I stroked his chest and plied him with kisses.

"Do you want me now?" My breath was hot on his ear as my fingers entangled in his dark golden waves.

"I want you, Claire, like a sinner wants his vice."

"What was it the Bard said, darling? 'Sin on your lips, O trespass gently urged. Give me my sin again' ..."

Our embrace was more fervent and led to an impassioned bedding which left both of us sated and breathless. When I donned my riding habit and pinned my hair up under my hat to go, I really did not want to part from Gilbert and said as much. Five years had gone without my friend, now lover, nearby ... and now five hours or even five minutes felt like an eternity.

XVIII

Gilbert brought a different side of me to the fore. Modeling for his paintings, many of which were suggestive, gave me pause at first. Eventually, I immersed myself in the project. It gave me time to think ... to think of myself as more than widow, mother or wife. I enjoyed the work; make no mistake, though, at times it was exhausting.

There were many afternoons when Gilbert would clean his brushes early and we would make love with an ardor that I had not known in many years. Gilbert's hands and tongue were magical at such times.

Love had come late to my life, both with Erik and Gilbert. I was surprised to realize how much of a tendresse I felt for my one-time majordomo; it was not too long before Gilbert gave up his rooms in Avignon and moved his belongings into my bedroom.

After Gilbert came to live with us, I put away our mourning garb. I told Veronique that it was time we looked like ourselves instead of crows. So, she had new frocks and shoes, as well as a yellow straw hat that I believe she would have slept in if given a chance, so fond of it was she. She also insisted that she wanted to have her hair look like Maman's, so Gilbert cut her black tresses at the shoulder blade and gave her a fringe.

"That's two ladies' hair I have cut now," he said to the solemn girl, who declared herself pleased with the result. Being called a lady did no harm, either.

As for me, I opened my trunks and took many dresses to the modiste for restyling. Fabric taken from narrowed skirts was used to gusset sleeves, to give them a fashionable leg-of-mutton shape. I sighed over many a piece; Erik had bought me a trousseau when we married, and each dress held a loving memory.

There was one piece that made me cry; deep in the bottom of my trunks was a blue ball gown with matching slippers. I held the gown close to me when I unpacked it; a wistful smile soon gave way to tears.

Veronique had been watching her from the doorway and came in shyly.

"Maman, what is the matter?" She sat down on the bed.

"Oh, ma petite," I smiled through my tears and joined her. "This is the first gift your papa gave me. It has been so many years now ... I loved him so."

My voice trailed off as I gathered my thoughts.

"I admired this gown in a window and he gave it to me. I had no idea then that we would come to love each other, and to have you." I shook my head sadly. "This gown looks so old-fashioned now, but it was the latest thing when your papa courted me."

"I am sure the dressmaker can fix it, Maman, as she did with the others."

I gently folded the dress back into its box, placing the slippers in with it.

"Perhaps one day, ma petite. For now, I'll keep it as a memory."

I next opened my jewel case and took out a box that opened to reveal a necklace and bandeau diadem made of beautiful blue sapphires.

"Papa gave these to you," Veronique said.

"Yes, ma petite, to go with that ball gown. One day, these will belong to you."

"I'd rather have Papa's violin," she replied honestly.

"You are Erik's daughter," I responded as I put the jewels away. "Music before all else. You are not yet ready for Papa's violin. When you are bigger, we'll talk about it again."

I came back to the bed and hugged my daughter tightly.

"How I miss him, Veronique."

"What about Monsieur Rochambeau," she asked, for that gentleman now stood in the doorway. "If he is, here why do you miss Papa?"

"I miss him, too," Gilbert responded. "Your maman will always love your papa, because he gave you to her. I am not trying to take his place."

This seemed to be just the right response. Veronique stood up from the bed and went over to Gilbert, opening her arms to offer him a hug. If he was surprised, he gave no indication; he merely held the child in his arms.

Of course, some of the women in town did not take kindly to Gilbert joining our household, even moving their skirts aside when I passed them on the streets . My time in London made me impervious. Likewise, the men who had once paid me court sneered at me. I didn't care, because at home I smiled and sang and whistled ... and Gilbert was kind to me.

XIX

One day, some six months after he came up the walk that first time, Gilbert took Veronique out to the garden for a private discussion. She was just coming up on six years of age. He later explained that, when he decided to propose marriage to me, he sought her thoughts on the matter. He emphasized once again that he was not trying to replace her papa, but that he wanted to make a life with both of us. Veronique's main concern turned out to be what she should call him, since he was not her papa. The two of them settled on the nickname by which she called him for the rest of his life: Beau-Père.

After shaking hands upon their agreement, the two conspirators came back into the house. Veronique announced that she was going to her room to play, and then had the temerity to wink at Gilbert.

Using his walking stick to steady himself, Gilbert lowered himself to one knee before me. I gasped aloud, for I knew then what he was about.

"Claire, I have nothing to offer you but my faithful heart. I will give you the labor of my hands, and all of the love I have held for you these many years. Please, will you do me the tremendous honor of becoming my wife?"

"Oh, my love," I whispered. "Yes, yes. I will marry you."

When I accepted the proposal, Gilbert pressed his cheek to my skirts and wept. I entwined my fingers into his dark gold curls and cried as well.

Clarice again reached for her pocket hankie. That was the most beautiful marriage proposal she'd ever imagined.

A long while passed before Claire picked up the book again. She wasn't reading as much of the journal as she had previously anyway; it was her last semester of high school and there were exams, dances and such. Of course, she still had her singing and riding lessons, but the round of activities for a senior girl in 1949 were huge. Plus, she'd turned eighteen; she was a real adult now and had to be thinking about her future. She couldn't decide between staying in town for college, or begging her parents to let her study opera -- maybe even abroad. If she were honest with herself, she would have admitted that she still hoped Jimmy Aaron might drop Eleanor Fountain and ask her to be his ... but she put those thoughts from her mind as soon as they appeared.

Still, she was fascinated with her family's past. One night, she decided it was time to read some more and to the devil with her homework.

XX

Gilbert took both of us to Paris to visit old friends, call on Monsieur Matisse with his paintings, and to choose my wedding jewelry. Before that, I still wore the gold ring, with its tsavorite garnet, that Erik put on my finger when we wed. Gilbert was very understanding when I cried as I took it off to keep in my jewel case; he held me and kissed my hair as I wept.

Veronique was thrilled to ride the train, of course, and to meet our friends.

My dear friend, Madame Antoinette Giry, leaned on her ballet mistress' staff to clutch Veronique's chin and remark on how much she resembled Erik. Antoinette was dressed all in black; her dark hair was pulled into a tight chignon, but her sparkling eyes belied her seeming severity.

"Gilbert," Antoinette said, extending her hand to him, "After so many years, you have the love you sought.'

He bowed over her be-ringed hand. "Yes, Antoinette. I am so fortunate."

"So," she said to all of us, "you must come to the opera tonight. Erik's box still goes unused."

"Oh, could we, Maman?" Veronique's head was filled with fantasies about the opera, thanks to Erik's vivid story-telling. She often asked to go, even though it was no place for a child.

"We brought no evening clothes, Antoinette," I demurred.

"Next time. You must promise me."

I agreed, and we left one friend's home for another's. In those days, manners dictated that a call last only ten minutes. I wished it were not so, but knew that we would visit again soon. We made our way to Zareh's home; he had been a friend of Erik's in those long-ago Persian days, and was dear to all of us.

Zareh's house was astonishing to Veronique; she goggled at the Persian furniture and rugs before taking up a place on a large pillow. Zareh, Gilbert and I drank glasses of thick Turkish coffee and reminisced.

"So, this is Erik's daughter." Zareh turned his jade-green gaze to where she sat quietly. *"Tell me, child, are you musical as well?"*

"I am learning the violin," Veronique responded. *I had taught her to speak when spoken to by adults and to confine her remarks, so she was rather direct.*

"And for fun, what?"

"I play with the kittens, or Maman reads to me."

Zareh went to another room and came back with a beautiful porcelain doll. He sat next to Veronique on the divan.

"This doll once belonged to a princess in Persia," he said. *'She knew your papa and me. She gave it to me for a daughter if I ever had one, but I think that she would like you to have this."*

The doll was beautifully painted, with a wig of real black hair and green eyes. Her costume was a long green tunic and trousers, and she had pointed leather shoes.

"What do you say, Veronique," I urged.

"Monsieur Zareh, what did the princess call her doll?"

"Her name was Khadija," he replied.

"Thank you. I promise to take very good care of her She is beautiful, and she looks like me with her black hair and green eyes."

It was many years before we learned that Zareh's beautiful gift had indeed belonged to the Persian khanum. Veronique was delighted to receive such a beautiful plaything, and Khadija became one of her dearest treasures.

"She is beautiful, Claire," Zareh said to me as Gilbert helped Veronique on with her coat and hat. "But she is solitary like her father. Have a care, ma vieille, that you do not encourage that. Let her learn how to be a child."

Veronique was so delighted with Khadijah that she barely noticed the time pass at the jeweler's shop on the Champs-Elysées. Gilbert bought me a golden ring set with a heart-shaped ruby and marcasites to mark our engagement, and matching gold bands for us on our wedding day. We celebrated with dinner in the Eiffel Tower restaurant.

Matisse accepted Gilbert as his student based on the portfolio of colorful studies. He would, of course, be expected to take lodgings in Paris by the time the new term started. As reluctant as I was to leave the security of my little farmhouse, I recognized that moving back to the city was inevitable.

Zareh offered to act as our agent in finding a suitable home for the three of us; with that worry off of the table; we could go back to Provence and make the necessary provisions to move north.

We were married by the mayor in Avignon shortly after our return to the country. I wore a green walking suit with tassels decorating the skirt, and a broad-brimmed green hat. Gilbert was wearing that self-same chocolate brown suit from his first visit; I believe we made a dashing couple.

XXI

We arranged for Estefan to care for our home in Provence until we returned for the summer, and packed up those things we would take with us to Paris. I encouraged Veronique to look upon the move as an adventure, telling her about the museums, the opera, and the school which she would attend.

"This is an important opportunity for Beau-Père," I explained. "He is going to be a great artist with his paintings, just like Papa was with his operas. We must go to Paris to help him succeed."

"Will I finally get to see an opera?" She was determined on this point.

"One day soon. Perhaps Madame Giry will have you sit backstage with her to watch. Would you like that?"

"Oh, yes, Maman! That would be splendid."

As Zareh had remarked, a solemn and solitary child. The sooner I could get her into a day school with friends her own age, the better. Having been reared by older parents outside the main village and thus away from other little ones had made her a tiny adult.

Zareh found a townhouse for us not far from Matisse's atelier, which was attached to the Salon des Beaux-Arts in the Eighth arrondissement. We moved our belongings into the fashionable Rue de la Madeleine address and I had once again to accustom myself to town. No more going about in riding breeches or calico gowns for me. While being an artist's wife might be seen as affording me certain freedom, I wanted to be as circumspect as possible. Having posed for the somewhat scandalous studies that earned Gilbert his position was one thing; being welcomed in Society was quite another, as I well knew.

So, it was off to the modiste for more new gowns; the woman I had favored before was still in business. I even surrendered the precious blue moire evening gown to be remodeled; Erik would barely have recognized the dress when it was finished. The décolletage was scandalously low; the bertha neckline was replaced with a narrow frill of black lace trailing up narrow shoulder straps. The voluminous skirt was now close in the front with a train and bustle at the rear. More black lace trimmed the sweep of fabric behind me.

The first time I wore the remade gown, along with the astonishing sapphire collar Erik had given me during our courtship, I was quite self-conscious. My hair was arranged over a "Marie Stuart" pompadour form, with a bunch of curls descending from the crown. The matching ear bobs sparkled by my face; I felt altogether top-heavy. Yet, as Gilbert and I sat in Zareh's box at the opera, I knew that I wore the highest style. My daughter was backstage with Antoinette, seeing how the magic was made; my husband looked elegant in formal white tie. Still, I could not help looking across the way at Box Five, from which I had once watched an opera with Erik seated out of sight behind *me, standing empty out of tradition and superstition. My life was not the only one still under Erik's influence though he had gone to the grave.*

XXII

This was an entirely new lifestyle for me. We lived in Paris during the winter and returned to Avignon in the summer. There were times when I felt a trifle guilty about that; so many of the artists in our circle lived in circumstances that I could not have tolerated even at my lowest. I knew that they did not always eat as often as they ought to, and I found myself inviting them over to dine just so that I knew they were fed. Henri Matisse was the only one in the group besides Gilbert to go home to a regular apartment and a wife.

I agreed to pose for the drawing class at the Salon; my work with Gilbert had taught me to hold a pose, and my time in the theatre had erased any morality attachments to seeing the human body. I think that some of the men were perhaps a trifle surprised when Moreau announced that Madame Rochambeau would be on the platform. I heard some mutterings about how "my wife would not be allowed up there," but I stood quietly, smiling over my nude shoulder at the students behind me as they drew.

I would love to pretend that life was always sweetness and light. I lived in fear of those days when the melancholia would strike. While I was never again as badly off as those dark days in London, there were still hard times.

Gilbert came back from the atelier more than once to find me curled up with Pierre on the parlor floor while Veronique read aloud to me from one of her storybooks. Each time, he would ease himself down to join us for a while before helping me up and settling me on the divan. I cannot explain why I never went there in the first place instead of lying down on the Turkish carpet, but that was where impulse always led me.

The divan and the bed were always arranged with good views from windows; Gilbert was insistent upon that point. He told me that he had read, "from the highest authority," that those who were ailing emotionally needed to have natural light and a window that could open to let in fresh air. He concerned himself with my health and well-being before anything else; no woman could have asked for a more devoted husband.

I pitied Veronique, whose childhood could not have been much with a madwoman for a mother.

Whenever I spoke of this to Antoinette Giry, she became most indignant.

"Mad? Cherie, you are not mad. Erik? He was mad, make no mistake." She smiled gently. "If loving and feeling deeply is madness, the world could use more of it. That is your only sin, if it can even be called such."

Erik was indeed mad, but had he not been made so by society? And why, despite my love for Gilbert, did I still miss the husband I had buried at Avignon?

I had no answer to that.

XXIII

I was so proud of Gilbert; his talent grew by leaps and bounds under the tutelage he received from the other instructors at the Beaux Arts. As much as I hated to admit it, I was glad we had returned to Paris. I knew that the mas would be well-managed in my absence. I was more protective of Erik's gift to me than I had thought possible. I looked forward to returning there during the summers, to be sure, but Paris was like a tonic to Gilbert and I delighted in that.

I saw Antoinette and Zareh often as well. I felt as though I were back in the bosom of family.

Veronique's continued solemnity, even as she made friends at school or took her violin lessons with one of the opera's orchestra, concerned me. Was it really Erik's heritage, or did it come from my own madness? After all, a child placidly reading to her mother while the adult lies in mental agony upon the floor was far from normal.

The nearby shopkeepers all came to know her, as she sometimes went to buy our bread from the boulangerie. I could not go walking with Veronique without someone telling me what a fine and grown-up daughter I had. I wished sometimes that she were more childlike, but still I was proud of her.

XXIV

In November 1905, Gilbert's earliest portrait of me, in the arbor at Avignon, was accepted into the Salon des Independents, a special exhibit to be sponsored by our emperor, Napoleon III. We were terribly excited, of course. Yet, when we went to the museum, we found Gilbert's piece, along with works by Manet, Picasso and many others well known to us by then, in a room of their own. They were off to the side, away from the main exhibits. The newspaper critic, Vollard, called the room the "cage aux fauves," the wild beasts' cage. He had no way of knowing that his slur would become the name of a movement: the Fauvists.

An American named Leo Stein bought Matisse's portrait of his wife, Amelie, "Woman in a Hat," as soon as the exhibition closed. Most of the other Fauvists did not fare so well in terms of sales, but their names circulated all over Paris. That show led to several more for Gilbert, and I posed for more paintings.

It was, in fact, Gilbert's growing fame that took us to San Francisco, California, in 1906. He was invited by the Mark Hopkins Institute of Art's director, an admirer of Fauvist paintings, to teach there. Having seen Gilbert's work during the exhibition, he wrote, inspired him to offer regular employment teaching aspiring artists.

Perhaps the exhibition was not so ill-fated as I initially thought.

I was frightened, of course; the little Provençal farm house where we summered was beautiful, and the first home Veronique had ever known. Erik had bought it when the English doctors told him he needed a warmer climate. The terra cotta plastered walls and blue shutters ... the arbored garden ... the barn and pasture with our horses and cats. How would I manage without those familiar sights and sounds? Even the Paris townhouse seemed impossible to surrender. At the age of eleven, Veronique could not envision any other world: nor did I wish to.

Estefan wrote to me periodically; he had stopped traveling with Ornella and was training horses in Marseilles. It was he to whom I turned, asking him to serve as the permanent caretaker of the mas, as he had done from time to time for us in the past. I trusted him to look after my precious animals, whom I could not take with us on this long journey and new adventure.

I worried about Veronique far more than I worried about myself. She was so much more solemn than the other little girls of her acquaintance, focused on her violin-playing, and she did not make friends easily.

Gilbert said that her tendency toward melancholy came from me. She was still a quiet child who preferred the company of her doll, books and animals to playmates her own age, even now that she was in adolescence. It was he who suggested we seek her out to talk about the coming move.

"Veronique," he said quietly, "there is no need to be afraid."

He put an arm around her in a gentle hug. As always, she enjoyed a loving snuggle from her Beau-Père. He smelled of bay rum shaving balm and the lavender blossoms tucked between his shirts in the clothes press.

"But why must we go, Beau-Père? Why cannot the Americans come here to study?"

"Oh, ma petite," he sighed. "How I sometimes wish for you and your mother that it could be so. She is frightened too, you know. She had hoped never to leave France again. But for me to have this chance to teach at a distinguished and important school like the San Francisco Art Institute, she has put her fears aside ... or at least kept them inside.

"She is more brave than she knows, ma petite." He grinned down at her, tweaking her long black braid and winking. "And so are you. Now, let us go to tea."

"But, Beau-Père! I want to stay here so that I may marry Monsieur Mo-"

He interrupted her; "It's done, Veronique. And you are far too young to talk of marriage to anyone"

XXV

So it was that, in February 1906, we boarded an ocean liner called "La Champagne" at Le Havre; that vessel brought our household to San Francisco. I was not a very good sailor and spent much of my time abed in the stateroom. Gilbert and Veronique would walk around the deck together, talking with other passengers. There were few families on our first-class deck, but she did find some companions with whom she could pass time. Veronique was more comfortable with adult company, generally speaking; even her classmates at the little village school had been kept at arm's length. Gilbert was fond of remarking that she was not a very childlike child ... and that she was very much her father's daughter in that regard.

The three-story house on Union Street into which we moved was furnished with things I had kept in storage while we lived in Avignon. The wrought-iron bedstead that I shared with Gilbert was replaced with a carved wooden frame sporting mythological figures; this had belonged to Erik. Most of our plain furniture had remained at the mas with Estefan. Many of the beautiful boutis quilts I collected came with us, so at least Veronique had her favorite coverlet: block printed with olives on a background of blue and gold. The colors reminded all of us of the Provençal sunshine, something else I missed in the fog of San Francisco.

Our house had a fenced-in backyard, with back stairs leading all the way up to doors on the second and third floors. I explained to Veronique that these were for servants and tradesmen to enter the house without being seen from the street. We had no servants in Avignon, so she was not familiar with this kind of arrangement. Veronique was charmed by the third floor dormer room that had doubtless belonged to a maid in a different time, and chose it for her own. There was also a carriage house, with room for two horses and a conveyance. Sooner rather than later, I would have to visit the horse trading market.

There was a gate in the fence, leading to the yard next door. This was the Kayes' house; the widowed Maeve, an Irish woman, and her son Michael lived there. Maeve's husband had been a merchant seaman; he died in the line of duty, and she had a small pension from his employer. Her plump figure and no-nonsense attitude both hid a heart of gold.

I hired a Chinese amah for Veronique. At fifteen years of age, she did not think she needed a governess, but I pointed out that someone must walk her back and forth to school. I still had bad days when I took to my bed, and Gilbert was up early to take the streetcar to the Art Institute. Lee Ming would help her dress, escort her to school and then to her violin lessons. It freed Gilbert and me, and gave her a friend to talk to.

Lee Ming was eighteen years old, but she had an air of gravity about her that gave me tremendous confidence that I had chosen well. She was intelligent and kind, and before long she was like a member of the family.

I desperately missed our horses; even knowing that they were in Estefan's capable hands was of little solace. I finally went to a livery at the corner of Kearny and Bush Streets to see their horses for sale.

The hostler was a trifle condescending, suggesting that perhaps my husband was better suited to examining "these critters" than I. It did not take me long to set him to rights as I stuck my thumbs into one horse's mouth bars to look at his teeth -- and pronounced him nearly a decade older than presented to me.

"Really, monsieur," I said with a cluck of the tongue as I petted the dear old muzzle. "You should not presume that my sex has rendered me ignorant."

He had the grace to blush to the roots of his hair, and to stammer out an apology.

I was truly taken with a tall, slender horse of a most unusual color. He was black, with a white blaze, and splash of white across his rump that was interrupted by black spots.

"That's an Appaloosy," the hostler told me. "Indian horse."

The Appaloosy (I later learned that the correct name was Appaloosa) snorted into my hand and took in my scent.

"He's right nice, ain't he?"

I was engaged in a not-at-all ladylike examination of the horse's legs, hooves, skin, eyes and teeth.

"He is indeed. If you would write up a bill of sale for him, and for that sweet old grey gelding you tried to sell me as a youngster, that would be splendid."

We agreed on a price and arranged for the horses to be delivered to the carriage house behind our home. Gilbert would understand ... I hoped. Horses should not be alone; they needed the company of their own kind.

The grey gelding was named Robespierre and the Appaloosa was named Talleyrand or Talley. I was so happy to have horses again, and rode Talley whenever I could. Robespierre had some light cart work now and then but was, for the most part, retired.

Clarice closed the book, which ended rather abruptly; she even paged through the blank sheets to the very end to make sure she had finished the entire diary. She had much to think about all the same. Gypsies had helped bring her own mother into the world! Clarice didn't know too much about the gypsies, or Romany, as her grandmother had called them. She couldn't help wondering what had happened to Ornella and Estefan; surely they were gone by now. That terrible Hitler had put gypsies in the camps along with the Jews ... she didn't want to think about it.

She eased herself down from the bed and walked over to study the painting on the wall of the dormer room that had once belonged to her mother. Yes, this was the first one: Claire, in the garden, rendered in colors never seen in nature. She could almost envision Gilbert, his eyes filled with love, capturing the scene.

And, goodness! *Grand-mère* was bold with her lovers. It was easy to see why Daddy had been a little worried about letting her read the books. For all Clarice knew, those books could have been considered illegal under the Comstock Act.

Chapter 10

Clarice was more curious than ever about her grandfather. She decided that she needed to read one more book before she took up the next journals: Gaston Leroux's biography of Erik LeMaître, which he had entitled *The Phantom of the Opera*.

Veronique was concerned at how much time Clarice spent in her room surrounded with the journals and other books about the period.

"Don't you think you should go to the school dance tonight," she suggested on a particular Friday.

"Mommy, I don't want to waste my time like that," came the reply. Clarice was at the kitchen table with a copy of Leroux's book, her grandmother's journals and a *Petite Larousse* dictionary to look up the occasional word she didn't yet know. "Besides ..."

Clarice stopped and redirected her attention to the books.

"Besides?"

"Jimmy Aaron is taking Eleanor Fountain, and I don't want to go with anyone else."

"Jimmy Aaron isn't the only boy in the word, Clarice."

"You don't understand, Mommy."

Veronique understood far better than she cared to admit, having been a solitary young woman herself. She decided it was time for some confessions of her own and went back to the trunk. When she returned, she carried a small stack of newer journals.

"Clarice, you can't shut yourself up like this."

"Mother, I don't think you understand," Clarice repeated.

"I understand all too well. I was once your age, you know ..."

Right on schedule, Clarice rolled her eyes.

"And when I was your age, I was madly in love with someone."

"Daddy, of course."

"No, not Daddy."

She had Clarice's undivided attention then, and slid the new stack of journals across the table to her.

Part III
Veronique

I

December 25, 1900

My name is Veronique LeMaître. I am nine years old. Père Noel brought me this diary.

II

My early memories of Maman are of a distant and unhappy woman. I had no idea, of course, that Papa was dying, or of how lonely she was in her quiet life. She loved our little farm, but company was rare.

When Tante Ornella and Oncle Estefan came to stay with us, Maman seemed so much happier. She was ever reserved with me, while Estefan, Ornella, Papa and, eventually, Beau-Père, made it their goal to coax a reluctant laugh from me.

Estefan taught me to ride at an early age, walking next to me. I loved horses; it was in my blood to do so. Most of all, though, I loved music.

All of my happiest memories involved Papa singing to me or playing the violin. Before his illness stole Papa's voice, he would sing anything from "Sur le Pont d'Avignon" to an aria for me. Maman's favorite was "La donna e mobile," from Rigoletto. Papa sang it often.

My violin lessons started at age two, with Papa presenting a tiny instrument and teaching me to finger a simple tune while plucking the strings. Bowing would come later, he said; I could learn pizzicato for now.

Sometimes Papa would take out his own unusual violin, made by Francois Chanot, and play a counterpoint to my plucking; those memories were the most precious of all.

There is no denying the peculiarity of my childhood. Maman, Papa and Beau-Père were part of a Bohemian set, to start with. Secondly, there was Maman's illness. Beau-Père forbade all of us from calling it madness or anything like unto it. He said that her illness was the body's response to heart-sickness.

I found that hard to comprehend as a child, although I understand it now. All I knew was that there were days when Maman remained abed ... or, if she arose, wore a night rail and a dressing gown instead of a frock.

Beau-Père said that I must be a big, brave girl and help Maman. I read to her, and sometimes I went to the café to bring food. Maman would tie coins into a handkerchief for me to carry, and then I would return with the order she wrote. I felt very proud on those occasions.

Beau-Père fawned over Maman; he always said he was the luckiest man who lived, to have a wife like her.

Was it really such good fortune? I believe he saw Maman through the most loving of eyes, but I sometimes wanted a mother like the rest of my friends had. Other mamans made tartines and hot chocolate for their children after school, or supervised cooks. They had "at home" days with guests or paid calls. Maman did those things, but not with any sort of consistency. Her ailment came on without warning; it was almost impossible to make plans.

As I got older, Maman's behavior became less confusing for me. As a child, I blamed myself for her crying jags and occasional bursts of anger followed by tears and an early bedtime for herself. I don't remember how I came to grasp that there was nothing we could really do to fix it.

Beau-Père had some correspondence with a Doctor Gachet, who was famous for what was called the moral treatment for melancholia. He advised good food, quiet rest and whatever meaningful work Maman could do. Beau-Père also read a great many books about emotional illness and followed the advice to the letter in order to do whatever he could to make Maman's life easier.

I was able, after a while, to tell when things were very bad for her. On the worst days, she could not tolerate corsets or stiff gowns. She would wear a soft wrapper over a flannel night rail and thick woolen socks instead of silk stockings and pretty shoes. She complained of feeling cold sometimes and added a shawl to her odd costume then.

We moved between Paris and Avignon with the seasons. I attended an all-girls' school when we lived in town; summers were spent in the country. As June drew near each year, I champed at the bit to be back on our little farm, with the horses and the cats. Maman always seemed happier in town; the country house held difficult memories of Papa's death. In town, she could forget for a little while.

Of course, it took me many years to understand that as well. I was eager to be back to the place I thought of as home.

Of course, all of that changed after the Salon des Independents. That was when I fell in love for the first time.

III

January 1906

I believe that the most beautiful man I have ever seen was Amedeo Modigliani. He came to Paris just a month or two before we left, and I remember seeing him at table when Max Jacob brought him to sup with us. His dark curls and deep brown eyes, his beautiful face; I was smitten. I didn't care that he was Jewish, Italian -- or that he was in love with an English woman named Beatrice (while living with a dreadful French woman called Jehanne). I was determined to marry him. Even though I was not yet fifteen years old, I was sure that he would wait for me to be of age. His skin was as fair as Maman's, who said that Monsieur Modigliani looked unwell. She invited him to dine with us often so that he might have a decent meal.

Maman worried about Beau-Père's friends at Lapin Agile and Bateau Lavoire, as they called their ateliers. She said they lived in horrible conditions, but I didn't know what she meant because she would not let me see. She also said that Beau-Père and Monsieur Matisse were the only ones of our circle who go to a real home at night. I told her that one day I would marry Amedeo and that we would have a real home. She smiled sadly at me; she did not understand that to be Madame Modigliani was my life's fondest dream.

I look back on those innocent thoughts with sadness because Maman was right. My beloved Amedeo was unwell; he had tuberculosis.

When Beau-Père announced that we were moving to the United States, to a place called San Francisco, I was horrified. How on earth was I to convince Amedeo that I was not a little girl ... that I should be his wife ... if I was all the way in the United States of America?

I did something I had not done in many years; I had a pretend tea party with my doll, Khadija, and an old stuffed horse called Josephine that Beau-Père gave to Maman before I was born. I tried to work out all of my fears and feelings as I sat with my toys and made conversation for all of us. Beau-Père overheard me, and we had many talks about my concerns after that. What if I never made friends? What if the Americans were as bad to Maman as the English had been?

And, of course, what about Amedeo? I had once donned one of Maman's walking suits and taken lunch to him at his atelier, in a desperate attempt to show him that I was a real lady. I was surprised at how small and mean his space was; it was dingy, and had hardly any furniture. No wonder Maman was appalled. Amedeo had kissed my forehead and told me to thank Maman for the food. I do not think he knew how much I felt for him. Or, perhaps he did and was just behaving like a gentleman ought to do.

It must be said that neither Beau-Père nor Maman made fun of my love for Amedeo, although it surely gave them pause -- to say nothing of consternation. I was absolutely sincere in my determination to marry Modigliani. However, my lot was that of a child's; soon enough, we were saying goodbye to both Paris and Avignon and boarding the ship that would take us to a new life.

IV

When we arrived in San Francisco, it was as though a weight was lifted from Maman's shoulders. I think that she felt Papa's presence ... or absence ... too much when we were in France. Her love for Beau-Père notwithstanding, she still had strong passions surrounding Erik. I blushed more than once when she let me read her journals of their courtship, and I had not been reared to prudery.

Mrs. Maeve Kaye, the Irishwoman who lived next door to us, watched out for Maman after she saw her go to the carriage house in her wrapper and socks -- without even her boots. Maman knew that her horse would never hurt her, but Mrs. Kaye worried that "the little French hen" would injure herself. She sent her son, Michael, through the backyard gate in our shared fence more than once to talk to her and convince her to go back inside. There was no condemnation or fear, but a kind of loving understanding that helped me to see Maman through different eyes.

I was not so different from the American girls at my school. I loved to read and was particularly fond of Louisa May Alcott's stories and the Bobbsey Twins books, even though the latter were "too young" for me. I still secretly had tea parties with Khadija and Josephine as my "guests." Where I differed most was my shyness. In hindsight, I suspect that it came from growing up in a house full of adults; I was unsure of what to say to other girls my age.

One day in class, we were asked to share something about our families. In a room full of youths whose fathers were soldiers and whose mamas had married young, my story stood out.

"My papa was an opera singer and composer; he died when I was little. My Beau-Père is an artist and he teaches at the Academy. My maman was a horse trainer in France."

Many of the children scoffed in disbelief, but Michael Kaye leaped to my defense.

"It's true, every bit of it. They live next door to us. You should just see her mama ride!"

I was awfully glad of the boy next door that day. It was not the first time he came to my rescue; nor would it be the last.

I had a Chinese amah who was barely older than me. I chafed at the idea of a governess, to say the least. In my own eyes, if no one else's, I was a grown-up young lady. I also believed that Amedeo would never marry me as long as I still had a governess; I sent him long letters to which I seldom received a reply, and those replies were always of the most gentle kind. In hindsight, I'm sure he was trying to let me down easily, although I refused to see it.

I was always fascinated by Lee Ming's clothes. She wore trousers, topped by a long embroidered tunic with slits at the side so that she could walk. She tucked her hands up inside long sleeves to keep them warm in the foggy weather, and always walked quietly in her flat, buckled shoes. She was eighteen years old, but had a dignity that made her old beyond her years.

She confided to me once that she was glad Beau-Père and Maman chose her to be my amah, because no one would marry a girl with "peasant feet" like hers. At the time, I thought she referred to her shoes; there was so much I did not understand. Later, when I met her mother and saw the tiny shoes into which she forced her bound feet, I rejoiced that Ming had escaped the cruelty. Yet, that was a sign of being a proper lady in Chinese culture. Because the law said that Ming could only marry a Chinese man, she had no hope beyond being a servant in what she prayed would be a kindly family.

V

Shortly after we arrived in San Francisco, Maman received a package from Zareh that made her weep; it was Papa's opera, "Don Juan Triumphant." Zareh had gone back to the opera house, he explained, knowing that some of Papa's belongings were still there. He took the score with him then, and wanted Maman to have it "for Erik's girl." There, in Papa's own untidy hand, was the most astonishing composition I had ever seen. This was nothing like the Czerny, Dvorak or Haydn works I had played at many a recital; it was a work of absolute genius. I ran for my violin, and played a few measures; the melody made my blood race.

"Please, Maman. You have to talk to Madame Ellis. I must play this piece at the next recital evening," I begged.

Maman eventually relented, and I pored over the score until I found just the piece I wanted to play. Madame Ellis found it confusing when I showed it to her; she had never seen its like either. Despite what she called the "unknown composer" (I had explained that it was my papa, but she dismissed that as "a child's fancy," for in her mind no modern composer could have created the work), she gave her blessing to present the new composition.

I played the piece constantly in preparation for the next performance. Maman and Beau-Père sat proudly in the recital room when I performed, but I could not help noticing the expressions on the faces of the other parents as well as my fellow students. They were not very well prepared for Papa's unusual piece, and the applause was polite despite what I knew to be a perfect performance. Only Maman, Beau-Père, Mrs. Kaye and Michael were truly enthusiastic.

After we returned home, I went upstairs and got ready for bed. I was upset and frustrated; I had hoped that people would recognize my papa's brilliance. Maman sat on the edge of the bed and talked with me for a long time. The opera had only been performed once, under duress on the part of the theatre's managers, and the sophisticated Parisian audience had not really known what to make of it either. It was clear that Maman expected no more from a group of American parents who were there primarily to hear their own child's performance, no matter how mediocre.

"It's unfair, though," I protested.

"Of course it is, ma petite. Unfortunately, you will find that many things in life are unfair."

She hugged me tightly, which took me by surprise. For as long as I could remember, Maman had been just a little distant with me, especially by comparison to Papa, our Rom family, and even Beau-Père.

"Your father would have been very proud of you tonight," she whispered. "Beau-Père and I certainly are."

I could have asked for no higher praise.

VI

One of my favorite things was when Maman and Beau-Père would have friends over for music and dancing. I would always play the violin for their guests, and then a little orchestra hired for the occasion would strike up popular dance tunes.

With carpets rolled up and furniture against the walls, the parlor became a ballroom. Though Beau-Père could not dance with her because of his bad leg, Maman never lacked for partners in the reels, waltzes and polkas. She was a great favorite with the soldiers, and had to quell many an argument over the dance card that dangled from her wrist. There were two or three gentlemen who were amongst her favorite partners, of course, but as long as there was a space left on that tiny card there were gentlemen vying to take it up.

I eventually learned that those soldiers thought Maman an adventuress because of Beau-Père's paintings. Still, I loved watching through the upstairs banister as Maman whirled through a dance in one of her brightly colored gowns with a smitten officer leading her in the figure. I would watch until Lee Ming made me go to bed.

I dreamed of the day when I would have gentlemen arguing over which dance was to be theirs, or who would accompany me in to supper. In those days, one did not sit with one's husband at *dinner parties; it was expected that people would socialize with others. In my fantasy world, Amedeo and I were a society couple giving balls and entertainments in a home on Nob Hill: never mind that he was in Paris with the dreadful Jehanne.*

San Francisco was more exciting to me than Paris and Avignon combined.

Another favorite pastime was when Maman would take me with her on the omnibus to the big City of Paris department store on the corner of Geary Street. Maman liked to buy our dresses there, as they came right from home, and we would have tea and cakes in the restaurant. I would wear one of my nicest frocks when we did this, and I felt very much like a grand lady.

Maman learned how to use a typewriting machine and went to work two days a week in the office of the Academy. I wished that she stayed at home like the other mamas, but at the same time her example told me that I need not live by society's whims and dictates. It was one of the most important lessons she imparted to me.

"Always be ready to make your own way as you can, Veronique," she said. "In so many ways, we are at the mercy of men. But there are always ways to manage. You do not need to be like every other girl. Be true to yourself; everything else will follow after that."

VII

April 17, 1906

Maman rushed me through my toilette lest we be late; I was finally going to attend an opera instead of watching it from backstage. Tonight, we would hear Maestro Enrico Caruso perform in "Carmen." At age fifteen, Maman and Beau-Père had finally deemed me old enough. I never understood their reluctance, given their fondness for music. It may have had to do with the themes, many of which were violent or dreadfully sad. Nevertheless, my time had arrived and I was going to make the most of it.

I was not only excited to attend the opera; Beau-Père had bought me a lovely evening gown from the City of Paris department store. It was a color called "San Francisco Green," with a black lace and bead overlay. I had never seen such a beautiful dress before, even in Maman's closet. I was wearing my skirts down from the time I turned fourteen, but day frocks were nothing to this.

Maman helped me arrange my thick, straight hair; my long, black braids were pinned up and looped so that my neck and ears showed. I lamented that my lobes were as yet unpierced, so that I was unable to wear any of Maman's earbobs, but she had promised that I might have them done when I turned sixteen. Tonight, one of Maman's necklaces completed the ensemble: a collar of emeralds that Papa had given her many years ago.

I looked and felt like a grown-up woman for the first time since my visit to Amedeo's atelier. At least I was wearing my own dress now instead of Maman's clothes. And the opera was amazing. Maestro Caruso reminded me of the times when Papa would sing to me when I was little. I could no longer bring Papa's voice readily to mind, which was unfortunate. At least I could hear other men sing and remember him fondly.

At five in the morning, on April 18, our lives changed yet again as an earthquake tore through the City I was coming to love so dearly.

VIII

April 1906

After the earthquake, one of the soldiers, a Major General Frederick Funston, declared himself to be in charge of the city. While our home, and that of the Kayes, was relatively unharmed, there was a great deal of looting going on by those who had lost everything — and those who sought to make a profit from those losses by selling stolen goods. Beau-Père stayed behind to guard our house, and Michael his, while Maman, Mrs. Kaye and I were moved up the way to the Presidio of San Francisco army base. We were among the lucky ones; we got to live in a little cottage rather than a huge tent with several other families. Maman had asked if we could share one with Mrs. Kaye; that counted as two families in one of the tiny dwellings, and the Army allowed it.

Maman also went to visit Lieutenant Colonel Torney, the commander of the general hospital, to see how we could all help out. Between the regular hospital and the field hospital, they were horribly short-handed. The Presidio General Hospital was the first to allow women from the Army Nurse Corps, and so Colonel Torney, whom Maman called Georges (his first name was the English George) accepted Maman's offer of assistance.

So, many mornings, Maeve, Maman and I would be on the wagon over to the field hospital in Golden Gate Park. We helped distribute food, write letters ... whatever was needed. Maman's staunch attitude in the face of horror saw her helping out the orderlies in surgeries. Maeve Kaye and I agreed that we could not have borne it ourselves; Maeve had never seen my Papa's face (which I must admit was becoming harder for me to recall to mind) nor heard about Philippe's burns. Maman was made of sterner stuff than one might ordinarily credit her. Beau-Père always said her frailties were well-hidden.

I think that many of the orderlies were half in love with Maman, to tell the truth. All the same, I once heard Maeve whisper to Maman that she had seen how some of them looked at me and that we would need to have a care.

The earthquake was a great social leveler. Nabobs and poor folk alike stood in long queues for food and coffee. On a particular afternoon, Maman and I were helping to serve food when some of the society ladies took it upon themselves to try to tell her how to behave.

They whispered about Maman as she ladled another spoonful of pale stew onto a plate and handed it to the next person in line.

"She's French. She may not know any better. We need to tell her."

Another scoop of stew, another quiet "thank you" from the recipient.

"Mrs. Rochambeau."

I don't remember the name of the society woman who addressed her.

"Yes?"

"Might I have a moment of your time?"

Maman wiped her hands on her apron. "Sergeant Pickett, would you be so kind as to carry on without me for just a moment?"

"Yes'm. I'll do that." His dark eyes watched her go, concern written all over his face, even has he spooned more food onto plates.

She joined the cluster of stern-faced women.

"Mrs. Rochambeau, you are serving in the wrong line. That's the line for ... " The pause seemed to go on forever. "Colored people. That's why Pickett is serving them. It's not right for us to be serving people like them."

The women nodded in unison, heads bobbing like so many chickens looking for scratch.

"Oh," Maman responded drily. "I am so glad you told me. You see, me being French and all, I must be awfully ignorant. Tell me, ladies, who else am I to avoid serving? The Irish, like my friend Maeve Kaye? The African men, like Sergeant Pickett? The Chinese ladies, like my daughter's friend and amah, Ming? French people like myself? Perhaps the Italians, like Signore Caruso? Please, do enlighten me."

The first woman spoke again.

"Please, don't be insolent. We're trying to help you. Colored people serve us, not the other way around. You'll give them ideas. The Bible says that the races are not to mix."

"The only idea I intend to give anyone, Mesdames, is that I can hand food to hungry people; which is something that the

Bible commands us to do. I do not recall seeing anything in that book that says we are only to provide food to those who look the same as we do. I volunteered to help Monsieur le Docteur Torney in any way I can, and today he has asked me to serve this stew. What are you ladies, with all of your 'thou shalt nots,' doing to help?"

Without waiting for a reply, Maman turned on her heel and walked back to Sergeant Pickett with her nose in the air.

"Miz Rochambeau, you don't want to make those ladies mad. They're officers' wives."

"I don't care if they're the Queens of the May Festival," she replied. She looked Pickett directly in the eye; neither her gaze nor that of the buffalo soldier wavered. "I am here to help all who come, Sergeant Pickett. All. "

"Yes'm. Now, let me get another bucket of this-here stew."

It was my turn to be awfully proud of Maman that day. Sergeant Pickett became our particular protector, always making sure that our share of the "earthquake stew" always had a little bit more meat in it. He also walked us back to our cabin each evening, making sure we arrived safely.

"Not all of the folks here are good, Miz Rochambeau," he said. "I won't let you or your girl come to any harm."

The cabin was tiny, with little iron bedsteads. We found that we were warmer if we put our ticking mattresses on the floor together and shared the heavy woolen blankets. Maman put a shawl over her head to keep her a little warmer, and soon Mrs. Kaye and I followed suit. Every little thing that we could do to make ourselves more comfortable was done. Union suits under *our flannel nighties were unattractive, but likewise kept us cozy during the cold night. There was no way to heat the wooden, box-like shelters.*

Unlike many, we at least had access to our belongings; Beau-Père or Michael could bring us anything we needed. Other folk had lost everything and had only the clothes on their backs.

It was about a month before the Army gave us permission to return to our homes. They had been deemed safe, and there were so many who needed the little wooden box where we had stayed.

Doctor Torney was very thankful for Maman and Mrs. Kaye's assistance; he wrote a lovely letter to Maman telling her so. The Army nurses still had their hands full, and would for some time, but it was time for the ladies to return home and look after things there.

I was happy to return to my own room, with its warm bed and my own creature comforts. Beau-Père held Maman very tight when we stepped off of the Army wagon that brought us, and our little valises, back to Cow Hollow.

"I missed you so," he whispered into her hair. They went upstairs together and closed the bedroom door behind themselves.

Clarice could hardly believe what she'd read: *Grand-mère* and her friend had nursed people after the Great Earthquake! The same grandmother who had been unable to rise from bed at times had gone out of her way to help other people in need.

It took a little while for Clarice to name the glowing feeling inside her: pride. Her family had done some amazing things.

It took some of the sting out of Jimmy Aaron not asking her to the dance ... and Billy Wakefield not calling as he'd said he would. She had not yet admitted to herself that the latter was a little more hurtful than the former. Clarice decided that she would mention it during her next lesson ... but only if Billy didn't mention it himself.

She turned to the next page in her mother's diary, only to find that a great deal of time had passed between entries.

IX

February 1907

Lee Ming invited me to celebrate the lunar new year with her family. She had told me all about the parade and celebrations that happened in Chinatown and wanted to show me. She also told her family that our family had given her such luck and prosperity, despite her peasant feet, she wanted them to be able to thank me. Permission was given, and Lee Ming took me on the street car to her home.

I met her mother first. Madame Lee's feet were smaller than a child's and she had difficulty walking. Lee Ming explained that all proper women's feet were bound starting from a young age; I am ashamed to admit that I asked her. I had never seen or heard of such a thing, but managed to keep my shock to myself. The majority of the woman's weight went on her great toe, as the others were twisted over into the arch of the foot. Apparently, Chinese gentlemen found the swaying walk that resulted from the binding most alluring.

Lee Ming insisted on helping me into her finest clothes before dinner; a red brocade robe with golden embroidery and wide sash across my bosom. She dressed my hair, putting it up in an elaborate, pomaded sculpture, and stuck a high comb with golden dangling beads in it. She powdered my face and rouged my lips; I did not recognize myself.

"You are my honored guest; it is lucky for you to join us."

When we came to supper, everyone was dressed in the same traditional fashion -- except for Lee Ming's brother, who wore a modern suit. Unlike uncles and cousins to whom I was introduced, he also had a modern haircut; the others still wore queues and skullcaps. Ming told me later that Madame Lee had slapped Song the day that he came home wearing his Sears, Roebuck suit and with his Western haircut. Madame Lee said that he shamed his ancestors. Song, though, wanted to be a modern man.

"My brother, Lee Song. This is Miss Veronique LeMaître."

"Samuel," he said, bowing over my hand. "I am honored to meet you, Miss LeMaître." His English was excellent and without accent; he had been born in California.

He was also quite handsome, with his smooth, golden skin and dark eyes. He was taller than the other men; I would later learn that Samuel and Ming were fathered by a white man who had passed away but left his claim income to Madame Lee. Law forbade them to marry, but could not prevent their love.

Samuel and I kept darting glances at each other over the supper table. He talked of his ambition to attend university and become a teacher. I could see him standing in front of a classroom and delivering instructions. His tone was polite and scholarly at all times.

Samuel asked for permission to call on me, which was a surprise. No one had ever done so before. I agreed. He suggested a date and place, and I promised to be there.

The first time we met together, I consulted both Beau-Père and Maman. They were not upset about me seeing Ming's brother; we were going to meet at a public restaurant called Sam Wo, which was opened in Chinatown after the earthquake. Beau-Père showed me Washington Street on a map, and helped me figure out which street cars to take. Maman gave me a new walking suit and hat ("It is time for you to have more grown-up clothes; you are almost sixteen") and helped me with my stubborn hair again.

I arrived at the restaurant a little bit before Samuel did, and sat with my pot of tea waiting for him. When he came through the door, I could tell he was nervous. Once we started talking, though, everything seemed to be fine.

Samuel ordered the food for both of us, speaking in Chinese; at one point his tone with the waiter became rather stern. He told me later that the man had said something insulting about me and that he had told him off over it. As we talked, Samuel put his hand on the table, offering it to me; I took it. I felt something I had never felt before, not even with Amedeo. I blushed a little bit as I looked at Samuel, whose eyes gleamed. I think that was the moment when we started to truly fall in love.

After dining on the unfamiliar but delicious food, Samuel walked me back to the street car stop. He helped me step up to the conveyance and bowed over my hand.

"I shall look forward to seeing you again, Miss LeMaître. I will send a note around to your parents asking permission to call."

I waved good-bye to him as the street car moved away, hardly believing my good fortune.

Clarice closed her mother's journal. There was one more puzzle solved; Samuel was the name her mother had murmured after she'd been told about the Chinese man at Sam Wo's — a restaurant her mother had evidently known about for some time.

Chapter 11

At school that week, Clarice visited the library several times. Her first time was to look up Amedeo Modigliani. She found herself looking at an art book that showed not only his highly stylized portraits of the woman her mother referred to as the dreadful Jehanne, but also a photograph of a slender, pale-skinned man, his shirt open at the throat, with thick, unruly dark hair. He was indeed as handsome as her mother's journals described; it was easy to see why the young Veronique would have had a crush on him.

The next trip saw her chatting with the periodical room ladies, looking for old newspaper clippings about the 1906 earthquake. Sure enough, there were the articles that talked about Caruso's performance of "Carmen," and how he was wandering the streets of San Francisco the next morning in his bathrobe after the Palace Hotel was damaged. There were also mentions of Frederick Funston, George Torney, and a good many other people named in her mother's diary. How funny it was to think of Veronique rubbing elbows with those important folk.

But it also gave Clarice pause as she thought about more recent history, and how long it had been since she had seen Grace Sakamoto. The two had been thick as thieves during elementary school, but when Grace and Mrs. Sakamoto came back from the internment camp at Tanforan, things felt different. Grace's demeanor had become haunted, and she no longer laughed as easily as before.

When Clarice mentioned to her mother that she wanted to see Grace, but was not sure how to approach the matter, Veronique came up with the perfect solution: they would use the dress shop where Grace and her mother worked to have Clarice's recital gown made. That way, the girls would have a chance to talk and make their own arrangements. She phoned the shop and made arrangements to look at patterns and fabric the coming Saturday.

After dinner that evening, Clarice went to her room for homework and journal-reading. She tucked herself into bed, Lucifer at her feet, and picked up Veronique's diary again.

X

Samuel and I saw each other often. He was always a perfect gentleman, taking me to supper somewhere in Chinatown, or for walks in the beautiful parks there. He was always reluctant to explain why we never ventured outside of Chinatown together, so I addressed the matter with Maman. It was she who explained the so-called Chinese Exclusion Act to me. One part of the law was that it was unlawful for a Chinese person (and anyone who had one Chinese parent was considered Chinese) to marry a non-Chinese person. White women who did so were forced to give up their American citizenship. As I was not a citizen, I did not see how this applied to Samuel and me.

Of course, this law was the reason that Samuel's own parents had not wed.

"Veronique," Samuel said when I mentioned this to him. "I love you. When you are old enough, I want us to go somewhere that I may marry you and not have to deal with this law. I do not know where that will be, but I have heard that some couples like us have gotten married in Mexico. Perhaps, in the meanwhile, the law will change. We must pray for that."

"I want to marry you, too, Samuel. More than anything."

He kissed me on the cheek. "One day, when the time is right, we will do just that."

So, we continued to see one another only in Chinatown. Still, that was not enough to protect Samuel. One day, after he had put me safely on the streetcar, a group of toughs assaulted him and told him to leave me alone ... to "stick with his own kind."

I didn't know it at the time; I only learned of it when Ming brought me the letter that said good-bye. Samuel was going to a town in northern California, Copperopolis, to manage the claim his father had left to his mother. It was the only way to keep both of us safe, he insisted. He promised that he would always love me.

I hurriedly scribbled a note for Ming to send back to Samuel, promising the same. At first, it was easy to keep my promise. But then my studies got in the way of writing regularly. Before long, I realized that I could not remember what he looked like. My letters became less and less frequent, and sometimes I only managed a picture postcard.

I think that Beau-Père and Maman were a little bit relieved, to be honest. While they themselves held no prejudices, Maman in particular knew how cruel the world to be to those who stood out from the crowd as Samuel and I surely would have done had we continued courting.

XI

It was just a few months later, on the occasion of my sixteenth birthday, that I received the gift I coveted beyond all else: Papa's violin. Maman gave it to me, along with a letter Papa had written before he passed away. The letter moved me to tears when I read it:

"My dearest Veronique:

"I have asked Claire to give you my violin, and this letter, on your sixteenth birthday. I used to dream of giving it to you myself, but it becomes clearer with each passing day that I shall not live to see that day.

"I don't know if I ever told you how I chose your name. Veronique comes from the Greek, bere nike. It means 'bringing victory.' You are my greatest triumph; no opera, no aria, no symphony could mean more to me. Your birth was the proudest moment of my life.

"Long ago, a young woman called me her Angel of Music. She believed her papa had sent me from Heaven to look after her. She was wrong. However, please remember that I will always watch over you from Heaven myself.

"With much love and the highest regard, I remain, your papa,

"Erik LeMaître"

There were tears in my eyes as I tucked Papa's precious instrument under my chin and drew the bow across the strings to play a requiem.

Chapter 12

Saturday at the dressmaker's was more difficult than Clarice had imagined it might be. Grace had changed so much; she wore thick glasses now, and her hair was cut short and curled in a permanent wave. She looked so much like her mother now, and no longer like the little girl Clarice remembered. Of course, Grace found her friend much changed as well, with her movie star hairdo and singing lessons.

Veronique and Clarice picked out a pattern, and Mrs. Sakamoto found the perfect fabrics. Grace and Clarice set off a ways talking about school, boys and so on.

"You always liked that Jimmy Aaron," Grace said. "But I don't think he ever liked you back."

"No, I don't think he did. He gave his pin to Eleanor Fountain. The girls in my restaurant club think she's silly. Oh! Grace, you should come with us next week to Sam Wo's and meet the restaurant club."

"I can ask about getting the day off, but I may need to work. I am needed here; it's graduation season and so many girls are having dresses made."

"I'm sorry, I didn't think …"

"No, please. Don't apologize. I will ask, and we shall see."

Although she wasn't sure why, Clarice was somehow sure that her friend would not come to the restaurant club.

She mentioned the situation to Billy the next day during her riding lesson.

"Well, she may feel uncomfortable being around people her own age after what she's been through, you know?" was his response.

"But she's my friend!"

"Those other girls aren't her friends, Clarice. Ask her to go somewhere when it's just the two of you, and I'll bet her tune will change."

"Speaking of going places, Billy ... why haven't you called on me like you said you wanted to?"

He turned his blue eyes toward her as they rode side-by-side.

"I didn't think you really meant that you'd want to go somewhere with me, Clarice. You're ... something special. And I'm just a guy who is trying to get through college by teaching people to ride."

"I don't ask just any fellow to my recital," she replied in an injured tone.

"Well, maybe I could come to your restaurant club."

"Or maybe you and I could go somewhere when it's just the two of us. Like a movie."

"All right. Let's go to a movie next Saturday night."

"It's a date! The Lumiére is showing 'The Wizard of Oz;' I never get tired of that movie. Can you meet me there?"

"I will be there with bells on." Billy could hardly keep the smile from his face.

Clarice was on cloud nine when she got home from her riding lesson. She hummed to herself through dinner and finally told her parents that she had a movie date Saturday evening.

"Billy's going to meet me at the theatre. Mommy, can you drop me off and pick me up?"

Veronique consented, and with that Clarice returned to her room to read more of the diaries.

XII

Spring 1909

Maman decided that nothing would do but she must have a motor car. She purchased a bright red Stanley Model R four-seat roadster, specifically because she would have no trouble driving it on San Francisco's hills or changing gears. All she had to do was open the throttle on the steam-powered engine.

And, of course, learn how to drive.

Michael Kaye came to the rescue again, sitting next to Maman and instructing her on braking, accelerating and the like. Maman opined that she would never love the car as much as she loved horses, but she enjoyed driving nevertheless. Her broad smile gave her away.

Despite Michael's insistence that cars, like ships, were female in nature, Maman called her automobile Napoleon.

"Even the Corsican was subdued by a woman," she said.

Before long, Maman was driving her car all over town. She had her duster, goggles, and driving hat, with all kinds of veiling, to keep dirt off of her clothes. Beau-Père never did learn how to drive the automobile; Maman threatened to get a chauffeur's uniform since she drove him everywhere. But the threat was always tempered with a smile that said she didn't mind at all.

For my part, I was very proud of Maman. When she set her mind to do something, she did it without hesitation. The bad days were fewer and further between, and I was better able to see the woman that both my father and Beau-Père had fallen in love with.

XIII

April 1910

Maman came home from her errands in a fury; she dropped a book on the hall table and went into her bedroom in tears. I followed her, asking what was wrong.

"It's all lies, Veronique. Every bit of it is a lie. It's the story the way she wants it told, but none of it is really him." She went into her room and closed the door.

Beau-Père picked up the new book Maman had cast aside and called me over. He showed me the title and told me to go next door to get Mrs. Kaye. I hurried to do so.

I knew just who and what Maman meant, of course. The author was a well-known French journalist, and noted for his overt fondness of a certain Swedish opera singer. He styled the book as an homage to her. Certainly, the author had called it fiction – but it wasn't. Not really. There were real people to be found in those pages, and the author was telling lies about all of them.

When I returned, I let myself into Maman's bedroom, followed closely by Maeve Kaye and Michael. Maeve took charge of the scene.

"Michael, you and Veronique go downstairs and make the tea. Mister Rochambeau, you let me take care of this little French hen of yours. No, no ... you stay here. The young folk can bring up the tea things."

I raised an eyebrow toward Beau-Père. I had what I was assured was Erik's stubborn nature and was unaccustomed to being dismissed. After all, even as a small child I had cared for Maman during times such as this

"Beau-Père, shall I?"

"Indeed. Do as Mrs. Kaye says. Both of you."

Michael and I went down to the kitchen.

"What's the matter with your mother?" Michael asked.

"She has fits that she calls madness, and Beau-Père calls sadness," I replied, flipped my long, black braid over my shoulder and out of the way. "It just happens sometimes, but today something set her off."

"What?"

"A book."

"Oh, come on, Ronnie."

"Don't call me that."

"Fine. But really? A book? What kind of a book?"

I cut her eyes at him over the top of the tea service. "A book about my father."

Michael poured hot water into the teapot and added the chamomile tea.

"Was your father famous or something, that someone should write a book about him?" .

"Infamous is perhaps a better word, Michael."

Michael picked up the tray and followed me out of the kitchen and back up the stairs. He intended to go all the way into Claire's bedroom, but the formidable figure of his mother stopped him.

"Oh, no you don't, Michaeleen. You'll not go into a lady's bedchamber; you got past me once today, but it'll not happen again. Give me the tray."

With that, Mrs. Kaye closed the door, leaving Michael in the hallway holding a copy of a French book, Le fantome de l'opera.

XIV

Christmas Eve 1910

It was to be a most festive evening at Lotta's Fountain; celebrate soprano Luisa Tettrazini had promised to sing. The occasion marked San Francisco's recovery from the devastating earthquake and a return to prosperity after so much deprivation.

We all bundled up to take the omnibus; the Kayes came with us, as did Lee Ming. Though I no longer needed a governess, she was a trusted family friend. She always gave me news of Samuel; inevitably, I felt guilty for not writing more often. I did not tell her that I could barely bring her brother's face to mind.

The diva sang "Last Rose of Summer" and "Auld Lang Syne," just two songs. She wore a white gown and hat, standing out from the sea of dark overcoats and tuxedo-clad musicians on the makeshift stage.

"How I wish Erik were here to hear her," Maman sighed.

Beau-Père kissed her forehead tenderly.

Lee Ming told me later that Michael had looked from the two of them to me with something akin to envy on his face.

XV

February 1911

When I read in the Chronicle that San Francisco was establishing a symphony, I wanted desperately to audition. Everyone said I was the best violinist they knew. Surely, with Papa's Chanot instrument and his "Don Juan Triumphant" score as my audition piece, I was as good as hired.

"It says men only," Michael responded when I enthused over the possibilities. "I don't think anyone will mistake you for a boy."

"Honestly, Michael. They must want only the finest musicians. I must throw my hat into the ring."

So it was that I auditioned, just as I planned. I played the solo from Papa's brilliant composition and waited for the proctor's decision.

"Miss ... Le Maître, is it? Yours was surely the finest audition we've heard today," came the voice from the pit. "Unfortunately, we cannot use you. Go home to your beaux and pretty clothes, my dear. You don't want to be a career girl; it's deucedly unfeminine."

Summarily dismissed, I rode the omnibus home in miserable silence. Why was the assumption always that women must want so little from life?

Around that same time, Maman got involved with a group of suffragettes. Having lived under the strictures of French coverture laws, lost everything because of them, and then being set free by Papa's letters giving her a bank account and a passport, she felt strongly about women's freedom.

California's suffragettes were women from all walks of life, and the same was true in San Francisco. The ladies welcomed Maman; I am sure that her work after the earthquake helped to open the door.

So, Maman would go off on her marches, a purple sash reading "Votes for Women" over her elegant walking suit. She maintained that the ladies should look their best when they were trying to change hearts and minds. I personally believe that her French charm helped change minds as well.

XVI

Ultimately, the ladies won; California's men granted suffrage on October 10, 2011, and our adopted city, while suffrage did not carry in town, was the largest one where ladies could cast a ballot. Most states still didn't allow it at all.

Sometimes I wasn't sure what to think about the whole thing. Beau-Père had some interesting thoughts about it.

"Your maman," he said, " feels best when she has something to care about."

He told me about how Papa brought her out of horrible melancholia by giving her an abused horse to help.

As I listened to the story, I thought about Maman's many miserable episodes. And yet, when strength was needed -- when the hard work was to be done -- she was tireless. The woman who sometimes could not rise from the bed could somehow keep going while others dropped.

I hoped that, one day, women would not only be allowed to vote all over the country, but also to play in the finest symphonies. I still felt a twinge of heartbreak whenever I thought about the ill-fated audition.

And then, in December, Michael told us all that he was joining the Army as a journalist. He'd wanted to be a newspaper writer for a long while, and this seemed like the best opportunity.

The Army would teach him what he needed to know, and he would gain experience writing all over the world.

I told him that I would miss him; he had become my best friend, and had been so helpful to all of us ... but most particularly to Maman, whom I was coming to understand better and better as I grew up.

XVII

August 1914

News from Europe was sporadic because of the war there. Maman occasionally heard from friends or loved ones; one of the most heartbreaking letters she received was from my Oncle Estefan. The horses had been requisitioned and there was nothing he could do about it. Josephine, Cesare and Angel, despite their ages, were taken by the French army. Only sturdy little Lladro had been left behind so that Estefan could do work on the property; the army said he wasn't big enough.

Maman wept every time she thought about her precious dressage horse pulling a cart and could only hope that the elderly animals were loved by their caretakers. Beau-Père was unable to console her.

"Josephine was my very life for so long, Gilbert," she said. "And now I don't even know where she is ... or if she is alive."

The stuffed black pony that Beau-Père had given Maman as a gift so long ago became a regular fixture on their bed, and I sometimes saw Maman cuddling the toy and whispering in its ear. It was heartbreaking. I wished Michael were here to tell me what I should do to help her, but none of us could ease her pain. I *found myself hugging her more than I had done previously, but I don't know whether it was for her or myself.*

Otherwise, life went on pretty much as usual. The United States would not get involved in what came to be called the Great War for a long while to come.

XVIII

April 1916

I met Leander Merritt at one of Maman's musicales the year I turned twenty-four. She and Beau-Père had long since allowed me to attend, and it amused me to watch the young soldiers make their shy way over to sign my dance card. They were somewhat in awe of Maman, because of her work after the earthquake, but her card filled long before mine. It was both a privilege and an obligation to dance with the hostess.

I wore short gloves to dance; my fingers were calloused from playing the violin. I had played Papa's precious instrument since my sixteenth birthday and was the envy of the little orchestra whenever they let me sit in. The instrument was made and signed by Francois Chanot, with his signature rounded body and extended sound holes. The scroll at the head turned backwards to better accommodate the tuning pegs. Papa's violin was rare, unusual -- and had the warmest, most beautiful tone I had ever heard.

That particular evening, I had joined the group to play "Bonaparte's Retreat," an old piece, but one that showed off my skill.

I noticed the soldier watching me; his wavy black hair contrasted with fair skin and blue eyes. He was one of the most handsome men I had ever seen. I felt a blush rise to my cheeks as he smiled and bowed slightly; he knew I'd seen him.

After the song, I put my violin away and rejoined the party. That handsome soldier approached me, a cup of punch in his hand.

"Lieutenant Leander Merritt," he said by way of introduction. "I thought you might like some punch."

"Thank you, Lieutenant. I am Veronique LeMaître."

"Please, call me Lee. How do you know the Rochambeaus?"

"Madame Rochambeau is my mother; my father died when I was young."

I felt stiff and wary in my manners; no man had ever affected me this way before -- not even Amedeo or Samuel. I was as awkward as a schoolgirl.

"May I sign your dance card, Miss LeMaître?"

"Veronique, please. And yes, absolutely."

He pencilled in his name for the last waltz.

"You are the most beautiful woman in the room," he whispered, his breath warm on my ear.

No one had ever called me beautiful before. My mother, with her gaiety and blue eyes, overshadowed my own solemnity.

"Until our dance, Veronique."

He squeezed my hand and stepped away to speak with Beau-Père -- from whom he received permission to call on me.

I must confess to a certain degree of cowardice; I still had occasional letters from Samuel, but I did not reply anymore. It had been ten years since he had moved to Copperopolis. He still held the torch for me, but I could no longer conjure his face to memory. I asked Ming to write to him and tell him about Lee; after that, the letters stopped.

I loved to visit Lee at the pilots' barracks on the Presidio. We were all carefully chaperoned, of course. Lee's particular friends, Lieutenants Daimian West, Tom Kimball and Erico Chan, were also pilots in the fledgling Army Air Corps. They flew the big deHavilland DH-4 planes, under the command of Major Dana Crissy.

The four soldiers took turns dancing with me to whatever record was on the gramophone when I came to call. We were always happy, it seemed; the privations of the post-Earthquake years were behind us, and the war in Europe was so far away that it wasn't quite real. Of course, Lee and his friends were training for duty in the air above those far-away trenches, but for right now we enjoyed the interlude and illusion of peace.

XIX

February 1917

I was standing on the shore of San Francisco Bay, flanked by Lee's friends and squadron mates as he flew the big deHavilland out over the water. I was so proud of him, even as I was afraid of him going to war. His squadron would be joining the Lafayette Escadrille in just a few more days, taking their great planes to meet the enemy over France.

It was Tom's muttered "uh oh" that alerted me to a problem in the air. Lee's plane motor was sputtering and he'd lost some altitude.

"Veronique, maybe I should take you home," Erico said, touching my elbow.

I shook him off.

Time seemed to stand still as Lee's plane stalled out completely and fell from the sky, crashing in a ball of flame on the edge of Alcatraz Island. I couldn't help wondering what the men in the disciplinary barracks thought, even as I watched the wreckage slide into the bay.

"Someone needs to go help Lee," I said, even as Tom and Damian put their arms around me to keep my knees from buckling.

"Why isn't anyone going to help him?" I sobbed. "Why?"

My keening must have been horrible to hear and see.

Erico took me home, just as he had wanted to do so that I wouldn't see my fiancé die. He handed me over to Maman after telling her what had happened. Maman and I sat on the floor together and she held me while I sobbed. For the first time, I understood the bone-deep misery Maman had demonstrated from time to time. It seemed as though my legs might never hold me up again.

"Shh," she whispered, just as she did with a frightened animal. She stroked my hair and rocked me in her arms.

In the days that followed, Lee's friends and squadron mates paid their respects The military funeral on the Presidio was held with all pomp and ceremony.

I felt as though my life and dreams were buried along with Leander Merritt. I could only think of myself as an old maid, most assuredly on the shelf now. Lee's squadron flew off to France; none of them came home.

Michael came home, after the armistice. He started at loud noises, and he seemed so much older than when he left. He wore gold-rimmed spectacles, and no longer seemed like the lighthearted friend who had gone away.

I suppose that the war changed all of us, one way or another.

XX

January 1920

Maman reluctantly surrendered the newspaper to me, as she knew that the article would be upsetting. My beloved Amedeo Modigliani was dead, a victim of tuberculosis. His common-law wife, the woman I still thought of as the horrible Jehanne, had gone home to her parents the day after Amedeo died -- and thrown herself from their rooftop. I found it in my heart to pity her, which was rather unexpected.

I went to my room and wept; it felt as though whatever remained of my youth had died along with Amedeo.

XXI

April 1920

I unpinned my hair nervously and sat in the chair, handing the photograph of Kiki de Montparnasse to the girl behind me. At age twenty-nine, this would be quite a change.

"Are you sure?" the beauty operator asked as she brushed out my thick black locks. My hair reached nearly to my waist.

I nodded. I was nervous, of course, and the snipping of the scissors so close to my ear did not help. The shears entered my hair at chin level and closed; a rain of straight black hair fell away. Before long I had a smart bob, shingled slightly at the back, with a fringe over my brow.

Maman took in my altered appearance approvingly.

"I like it," she announced. She unpinned her hair, still thick but now falling in waves of white. Like mine had just hours before, her hair rippled to near her waist. She combed it out, and contemplated her reflection. "Take me to this beauty shop of yours."

Indeed, Maman proved that she was still something of an adventuress. She not only bobbed her hair but bought and applied a bright red lipstick. When Beau-Père saw her, he goggled.

"Claire, my love, do you remember that night in Paris when you cut your hair? You look just as beautiful now as you did then, with the fires of anger blazing in your eyes." He rested his hand on the back of her neck. "I am so fortunate to have you."

Maman caressed Beau-Père's temple, where the dark gold of his hair was silvered with age. "Mon amour," she whispered.

I could only hope to have a life as happy as theirs.

Michael complimented my new hairdo as well: "The girls in France have been wearing their hair like this for a little while; you look very smart and up-to-date," he said one night as we chatted over the fence.

"Do you really think so?" I could feel myself blushing, and was glad of the dim outdoor light.

"Yes, I do. You look lovely."

He reached across the fence and touched my cheek. I leaned in to his touch, which I think surprised both of us.

"I need to go check on Mother," he said, drawing his hand away. "I'll see you tomorrow, all right?"

With that, he was gone ... while I stood in the twilight wondering what had just happened.

XXII

July 1922

Maman loaded us all into her bright yellow Packard touring car so that we could go to the seashore at Santa Cruz. We stayed at the brand-new Bahia Hotel, just across from the sand and the boardwalk. She was tired from the long drive, but joined us all at the salt water natatorium for a swim that first evening. She took long walks on the sand, and wrote a great deal in her journals.

She confided in me that, while she loved Beau-Père with all her heart, sometimes she wished that Papa was still with her to see what a fine young lady I had become ... and, perhaps, just for a few moments, to walk with her on the seashore and feel the sun on his face.

It was later that night when she showed me her journals. In fact, she had written in one just that day, a poignant letter to my father that spoke of walking on the sands of France's warm coast, their faces toward the sun and eternally young. I barely remembered my father; Beau-Père was the man who helped Maman raise me. Until then, I had no idea how much she missed and loved Papa after so many years, and it gave me food for thought.

Michael and I had been keeping company since that moonlit evening. I had never fully given my heart to him after Leander, although I knew that he had eyes only for me. I felt as though loving someone else would be disloyal. That weekend at the seashore helped me realize that loving someone else did not take away what one felt for the new love; it merely meant that one had a heart big enough to love more than one. The parallels between Michael and me and Maman and Beau-Père were deeper than I'd realized; both men had always been there, on the sidelines, to pick up the pieces around the women they loved without promise or hope of reward. It spoke to their depth of character.

So, Michael took me to dime matinees or came over to supper. I realized that, at the bottom of my heart, I really had loved him all along. It was a quiet, steady love without the tumult in my heart that came with Samuel or Lee, but it was there. It was, in fact, just like Maman and Beau-Père, I realized.

It was not long after that weekend before I made love for the first time in my life ... with Michael. I could not have imagined an experience more natural than what we had together.

XXIII

June 1925

Michael took us all out to the picture show, thinking we might enjoy seeing "The Phantom of the Opera." Lon Chaney looked nothing like my Papa, although he looked very much like the descriptions in the Gaston Leroux book that had upset Maman so very much all those years ago. Maman also said that Mary Philbin was even more silly than Christine Daae had been, but that perhaps it was unkind to speak that way of people long dead.

Many women in the theatre screamed when the mask was pulled from Erik's face, and no small number fainted. I was embarrassed for them. Beau-Père asked Maman repeatedly if she might not prefer to go home, but we all stayed until the very end.

"I cannot for the life of me decide why they would show Erik murdered by an angry mob. It's even less true than that silly book of Leroux's," she complained quietly in the car.

XXIV

June 1927

Maman came out of her bedroom one morning, more than a trifle distraught.

"Veronique," she called through my door. "Would you please go next door and get Michael?"

I stumbled out, pulling a dressing gown over my nightdress.

"What do we need him to do? Can't I just phone him?"

"No, my dear. I will need the phone. Beau-Père passed away in his sleep, and I must call the coroner's office."

She looked so lost and alone; all I could do was wrap my arms around her briefly before literally running to the Kayes' house.

When I came back with Michael, and the indomitable Maeve bringing up the rear, Maman was sitting in the parlor, holding Beau-Père's blue-handled walking stick. She wept unashamedly, until she realized we were there. Then, she took out a handkerchief to dry her eyes.

"The coroner will be here shortly," she said. "I have Beau-Père's will, and we will get through this. I cannot believe I am burying another husband."

Maman seemed to collapse in on herself then. Maeve sat down next to her on the sofa and engulfed her in a hug.

"Let it all out, my little French hen. We will be your family now."

XXV

June 1930

After Beau-Père passed away, Maman started talking about France again. She wanted to go back to her home in the countryside. Even though the horses were long-gone and she hadn't seen the property in decades, it was all she could talk about.

Michael asked me to marry him, and I said yes.

The country was in what was called a Great Depression. Paying calls no longer meant going out for large dinners; no one had the money for that. We were well-supported because of Beau-Père's paintings, but Maman was frugal. There always seemed to be enough extra to give sandwiches to the men who came to the back door begging for odd jobs or food; Maman made sure of that. She also kept a dish full of coins on the kitchen counter; sometimes a dime or nickel made a huge difference to the hungry.

The day after we married, Maman sent a letter off to France. She would not tell any of us what it said until she heard back, she told us. It was not like her to be so mysterious.

When at last Maman got her letter back, she told Michael and me that she was leaving us the house. She had arranged for a friend to take her back to France, she announced: back to Erik. Beau-Père, she said, belonged to San Francisco; she wanted to go home.

We all knew what she meant.

On the day that Maman was scheduled to go back to France, an elegant Packard limousine pulled up in front of the house. A tall, handsome man with thick white hair swept back from his forehead got out and settled his hat on his head. He rang the bell at the front door and I opened it.

"I am here for Claire Rochambeau," he said.

Maman was tapping along the hallway floor, leaning on Beau-Père's blue-handled walking stick. The past few years had seen her grow physically frail, and she needed the cane much as he had.

"You are here," she said.

"I'm her daughter, Veronique," I said, letting the stranger walk past me and watching him kiss Maman on each cheek."

He turned around. "It is not possible. Veronique is a tiny child. Surely the great lady before me is not the little girl whom I tossed in the air just to hear her laughter? Who I taught to ride on the back of a spotted horse?"

I narrowed my eyes briefly, and then I could see him as a younger man: a man with long, black hair and a thin mustache.

"Oh, Oncle Estefan!" I threw my arms around his neck. "You must meet my husband, Michael. We have so much to talk about."

"Yes, my dear. I promise. And then, I will take your Maman home."

Chapter 13

Clarice closed the last of the books and sighed. She went to find her mother and father. Michael and Veronique were in the kitchen, drinking warm mugs of tea.

"I've finished the diaries, Mommy."

"Well, now you know." Veronique took Michael's hand.

Clarice had sometimes been embarrassed at how her parents showed so much affection to each other; she understood better what they had been through before marrying later in life. She had always thought of them as older people, and had never considered that they might once have had the same feelings, hopes and fears that she herself faced as a young person.

It was a few minutes before she replied.

"They had amazing lives, didn't they?"

Veronique nodded.

"I wish I had known your grandfather, Clarice. But I'm so glad to have known Claire and Gilbert. Your grandmother was one of the bravest women I knew." Michael adjusted his glasses.

"So, what happened after Estefan took Claire back to France?"

"She was seventy-two years old when she went back home," Veronique replied. "She lived out the rest of her days at that little house in Provence. We had letters from her regularly; she said that sometimes she felt Papa's presence there. When she died in 1936, it wasn't safe for us to go for the funeral. Estefan took care of everything. His son still keeps up the house; it belongs to us now."

"She died when I was five, then. I remember receiving money from her each year for birthday and Christmas, and you always put it away for me."

Michael took a little book out of his shirt pocket and handed it to Clarice.

"Yes, we did. Your mother and I decided that it was time for you to have this."

"A bank book?" She thumbed through the pages, her eyes widening. There was surely more here than what *Grand-mère* had sent her in five years.

"She left a good deal of money to you, and we had Estefan wire it to the bank."

"We must go to Provence." Clarice said. It was not a question, but a declaration. "And we must see Paris as well. I must see where *Grand-père* lived."

"They lived in many places, Clarice."

"Yes, but I want to see the *Opèra Garnier*. I'm the Phantom's granddaughter."

But first there was the recital to get through. Clarice rehearsed and rehearsed, and finally the big day came. She had the beautiful new dress made by Grace Sakamoto: black lace, with a full skirt, real silk stockings and soft leather pumps.

When they arrived at the rented hall, Clarice looked around to see whether Billy had come. She didn't see a cowboy anywhere and guessed that he had not been quite straight with her when he'd accepted the invitation.

She followed Mommy and Daddy inside the auditorium; there were a great many people there already!

"Clarice!"

It was Billy, behind her. When she turned around, she was surprised! He wore a handsome suit and tie, and a lovely fedora hat. He really was a remarkably good-looking fellow, Clarice realized. He handed her a box from the florist, and she opened it to see a corsage of violets.

"I hope you'll wear them," he said, looking deep into her eyes.

Mommy and Daddy turned around to see what was keeping Clarice.

"Billy!" Mommy said, at the same time Daddy said "William!"

"Professor Kaye, Mrs. Kaye," Billy replied.

"William is one of my students at the college," Daddy was explaining to Mommy. "He has the makings of a fine newspaper man."

Billy turned red at the praise. "Let me help you with the flowers," he offered to Clarice, pinning them at the shoulder of her dress.

"They're perfect," Clarice said.

When it was her turn to sing, Billy clapped and cried "Brava!" louder than anyone else. And when she stepped down from the stage and into his arms, she knew that she was in love with him. Perhaps she always had been — just like Mommy had been with Daddy. Billy would keep her safe from any storm.

Epilogue
Clarice

Chapter 14

June 1950
San Francisco

The week that Billy graduated from college, he found a job with the *San Francisco Chronicle*. He also asked Clarice to be his wife, and she said yes. She wore a simple diamond solitaire that she decided was much nicer than Eleanor Fountain's had been … and was a little ashamed of herself as soon as she had the thought.

To celebrate their engagement, Michael suggested that the family visit Sam Wo's Restaurant in Chinatown. So, there they were: Billy's widowed mother Helen, the redoubtable Maeve Kaye, Michael and Veronique, Billy and Clarice, ordering chop suey and egg foo yung. It was like a big meeting of the Saturday Restaurant Club, but with more laughter.

They didn't pay much attention when another family came in … until Michael stood up and went over to the table to shake hands with that same older Chinese man who had addressed Clarice in the restaurant before.

"I'm so glad you were able to come, Mr. Lee," he said. "Please, come and speak with us."

Veronique's jaw dropped. "Samuel!" she exclaimed.

"Yes, it is I. Please, meet my wife, Martha, and our children." Here he hesitated a little before introducing them. "This is our son, John, and our daughter ... Veronica."

Veronique somehow managed to keep her surprise from showing on her face. That Samuel had named his daughter after her was unexpected, to say the least.

Samuel continued. "Ming will be joining us soon; I know she will want to see you. Mr. Kaye, thank you so much for inviting us today."

"Daddy, how did you find them?"

"There are advantages to having a newspaper man in the family," Michael winked. "William and I put our heads together and sought out Chinese families who had survived the '06 earthquake so that he could write about their experiences. It didn't take me long to find the Lee family, with their connection to you."

When Ming came in, a little bent from age, but still wearing the wide-sleeved tunic and trousers that Veronique had found so fascinating, there were more hugs and laughter all around. She sat next to Clarice, saying "I must tell you stories about your mother when she was a girl. I think you will be surprised at the things she got up to."

"You must promise to tell both of us," Clarice replied, Billy's hand in hers. "I didn't realize how important my family's stories would be until I started to learn them."

"And you, my child, must always be looking forward to writing the next chapter."

Glossaries

French Words and Phrases Found in This Book

Aubergine - Eggplant
Au revoir - Goodbye
Barbe et moustache - Beard and mustache
Beau-Père - The nickname Veronique gives to Gilbert literally translates as "handsome father." Nowadays, it is used in France to denote either a stepfather or a father-in-law.
Boutis - colorful Provençal quilts, usually made from block printed fabric, with complicated stitching patterns
C'est - It is
Charges d'affaires - Business manager: the person who controls someone else's purse
Courgette - Summer squash
Demi-monde - Literally, "half-world." This was the part of society that was considered less than appropriate
Gardian - French equivalent of a cowboy
Grand-mère - Grandmother
Ma cherie - My darling
Ma petite - My little one

Mas - a Provençal farm house
Maman - Mama
Mes amis - My friends
Mon amour - My love
Mon vieux/Ma vieille - My old friend
Provençal - From the region of Provence
Trufficulteur - A truffle dealer

Romany Words and Phrases Found in This Book

Ashen devesha, Romale - May you remain with God
Bokoli - thick pancakes stuffed with small pieces of meat.
Ferari - Ironworkers/tinkers *Gadje* - anyone who is not of the Rom
Gadje gadjensa, Rom romensa - Gadje with gadje, Rom with Rom
Grastari - Horse traders
Latcho drom - "Safe journey"
Me som - "I am," for introducing and giving one's name
Nais tuke - Thank you
Pachiv - Ceremony or celebrations to honor special guest.
Pachivaka djili - Pachiv song
Perina - Thick quilts
Plal - brother
Rom - Husband
Romni - Wife
Vardo - Horse-drawn living wagon
Zhan le degesha tai sastimas - Go with god and in good health

For more information, please visit http://wwwz.arnes.si/~eusmith/Romany/index.html.

About the Author

Books by internationally published author Sharon E. Cathcart provide discerning readers of essays, fiction and non-fiction with a powerful, truthful literary experience.

A former journalist and newspaper editor, Sharon has been writing for as long as she can remember and always has at least one work in progress. Her primary focus is creating fiction featuring atypical characters. You can learn more about Sharon's work by visiting her Facebook page, http://www.facebook.com/sharon.e.cathcart, or her website, http://sharonecathcart.weebly.com.

Be sure to check out these other titles by Sharon E. Cathcart:

In The Eye of the Beholder: A Novel of the Phantom of the Opera
Les Pensées Dangereuses
Sui Generis
You Had to Be There: Three Years of Mayhem and Bad Decisions in the Portland Music Scene
2010 Hindsight: A Year of Personal Growth, In Spite of Myself
Around the World in 80 Pages
Some Brief Advice for Indie Authors
The Rock Star in the Mirror (or, How David Bowie Ruined My Life)
Through the Opera Glass
His Beloved Infidel
Brief Interludes
Clytie's Caller
Whispered Beginnings: A Clever Fiction Anthology (Contributor)
Live Life: A Daydreamer's Journal (Contributor)
Bestseller Bound Short Story Anthology, Vol. 1, Vol 3 and Vol 4. (Contributor)
Born of War ... Dedicated to Peace (Co-author)

Made in the USA
San Bernardino, CA
03 May 2014